I0785618

MIDNIGHT VICTORIES

MIDNIGHT VICTORIES

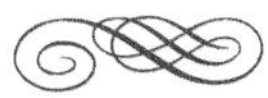

Midnight Whispers Series Book One

L.K. LATHAM

L.K. Latham

Contents

Dedication   vii

1   1

2   13

3   36

4   74

5   91

6   104

7   117

8   133

9   153

About The L.K. Latham   170
Midnight Loyalties   171

Copyright © 2000 by L.K. Latham

All rights reserved. No part of this book may be reproduced in any manner
whatsoever without written permission except in the case of brief quotations
embodied in critical articles and reviews.

For my sweetheart of a husband who said, "Go for it."

Edited by: James Goolsby
Cover image by: Natalie Narbonne -
https://www.originalbookcoverdesigns.com/

I

On a street in front of a house with a tree near the corner where the stop sign lies on the ground sits a car. The motor is running, lights and radio on, door open. There is no one on the street. The lights in the houses are dim and few. A dog barks at a seagull scavenging an overturned trash can. Lightning over the Gulf is too far away for anyone to care. If no one is around to hear the late-night DJ, does anyone listen?

Victory has a price,
though she stands tall and proud.
In silent condescension, she offers you the laurel.
But the vines of time have wrapped her sword
and no one seems to notice.
Who can meet that gaze and not hear the battle drums?
The shadows lengthen before the dawn,
but you know this song.
I'm Mary Midnight. You're at KMND Galveston.
Somewhere between night and day, the players take their sides.
And Victory stands, waiting.

Kiss my ass!" Avery slammed the door behind her. Glass beakers rattled. One teetered precariously close to the edge of the shelf.

"Bitch," snorted Dr. Milton Keats as he bent over his microscope.

John looked at Keats and rubbed his head, a headache forming behind his eyes. He fought the urge to punch Keats and followed Avery into the corridor. He watched her long, lean figure as the elevator doors opened for her as though she entered the elevator everyday at this time. He lifted his arm to signal her to wait, but the darts flinging from her eyes stopped him.

John felt her electric wrath in the elevator when it returned for him. He hurried but tried not to look like he hurried out the lobby the joined the towers of Sealy Hall. As the sliding glass doors closed behind him, he halted. With a swoosh hot, humid air sprinkled with stale tobacco, sweat, and salt pushed against him. After a deep breath, he moved toward the parking garage past the driveway and around a small artificial hill with five oaks, walking as fast as the heat allowed. It was too hot to hurry.

Avery stood next to the Coke machine by the garage elevator. She held her phone in her hand as though timing how long it took John to catch up to her. She smirked when she saw him and leaned close to the Coke machine, as though expecting the coolness of the inside to flow out to her.

"Avery."

Beads of sweat formed at his temples by the time he reached the shade of the garage. He loosened his tie, a habit he picked up since arriving in Galveston. He discouraged sloppiness. An officer must always set the example, but the Gulf Coast summer was winning its battle with etiquette. It was late June.

He took a minute to compose himself, rubbing his eyes. Avery leaned into the red glow of the Coke machine, giving her skin an inhuman radiance. Avery stepped back and searched her pockets.

"Don't you ever sweat?" he asked.

"It's not hot enough to sweat, yet. Give me a quarter."

Her voice still had that edge. He found a quarter in his pocket and gave it to her.

"I'm sorry…"

"Don't you apologize for that jackass! I've had enough of his crap.

You can find someone else to coordinate your project. I'm sure if you look hard enough you'll unearth some dweeb who can blow the way he wants."

"It's not that simple." He lowered his voice. "Security is tight on this project. I set up a system—"

"Fuck the system." She punched the Coke button. *Crack!* "Pardon my French, but I've had it. Maybe you have to work with Dr. Kiss-my-ass, but I don't. I've done all I can to make your job a little easier. No more. It's bad enough working at keeping his hands off me without his ogling every woman I send in there. I've worked with these women a long time. They trust me. I'm not putting them where they'll be groped and drooled over. It's up to you, now. I'm out of here."

He leaned against the brick wall of the elevator shaft and closed his eyes. She was right; contesting the point was useless. They both knew Avery couldn't quit. She signed the contract and security required no substitutions of staff, but she could raise attention to a classified project. As chief of security, he would not let that happen, even if she objections were justified.

"Things are changing. I need to increase security. At least one guard in each lab at all times?"

"Do they understand what they're guarding?"

"They're good people." John said. "I handpicked my team. They know what they're doing."

"I'll protect my people, making a formal complaint if I have to."

She lifted her Coke can for a long swallow. She looked like a movie star in a commercial. John expected music to fill the garage and dancers to leap down the stairs in unison.

He could see her calming down, but her eyes still burned. "It's late. I'm going home."

He remained leaning against the wall, trying to absorb the coolness of the brown brick. She glided effortlessly into the stairwell, led by the stride of her long legs, the rest of her body following, swaying gently left then right. He sighed.

She stopped before disappearing into the stairwell and turned back to him. "Dinner's at eight. Clara will want you there early."

She moved out of sight.

John felt his face redden. Whenever Avery decided a conversation was over, she brought up Clara — the one topic John never took in stride. No one bested John. In over twenty years of service, his sharp manner and ability to take control of any situation made him superior to his peers and gained him the reputation as the one man for tough and delicate missions. This assignment, however, challenged his skills and imagination to their limits. And now he had a weakness—one which Avery exploited with ease, sometimes shamelessly.

Thinking of Clara, John relaxed, despite his intentions. He pictured Clara sitting at Avery's desk. It was early May, John had been in Galveston only a few days when he walked into Avery's office and saw Clara sitting at the desk. She leaned back in the chair, her bare legs relaxing on the desk as she glanced through the stacks of papers, a violation of security, but before he could speak she looked up and smiled.

"Why you must be Colonel Espinoza. Avery's told me all about you. She said you might come by. Here's the report you're looking for. She didn't say you were a looker."

"You shouldn't be in here without clearance."

"Oh, that's okay. I'm not staying. Besides, I'm the closest thing to family Avery's got. And if you can't trust your family, what's the point? There's nothing on this desk that I don't already know about anyway." She laughed at the stare he gave her. "This is a small island. You don't think secrets aren't buzzing around here all the time, do you?"

He could not speak.

"I'm being rude." Standing up, she reached for his hand. "Clara Lucas. Avery and I have been best friends since high school, and now we're housemates. I just came by to pick her up. You ought to come around to the house tonight. You're from the Midwest or something like that, aren't you? Well, nobody's perfect. Come to dinner. Dinner on the beach is the best way to beat the summer heat. Daddy's bringing over some shrimp tonight. Mamma called to say he docked this morning with a good catch. There'll be plenty. We'll eat about eight, but you can come out early if you'd like. I'd like."

She looked past him and walked out the door without waiting for a reply. "Well, speak of the devil. Here she is. I'm sure Avery will be tickled that you're coming to dinner."

That night he went to Avery's house for dinner. He stayed for breakfast. In a few hours, Clara dispelled his preconceived notions of a good woman. All men fantasized what it would be like with a woman like Avery; she was statuesque, beautiful, and had an otherworldly quality that enticed fantasy. Clara was different. Her short-sleeved shirts exposed muscles formed from dealing with animals at her veterinarian clinic. Her mousy hair curled about her head with as much energy as her eyes contained. But her expression was genuine and her air sincere. She captivated anyone she set her mind to.

He discovered that the energy Clara demonstrated in their first meeting did not diminish in the evening. She moved from kitchen to living room to beach without missing a detail of the conversations. It was easy to see why she and Avery were friends. While Clara did everything enthusiastically, Avery was mellow and flowed along with what was happening. At some point Avery went to bed, leaving him alone to help Clara wash the dishes. Now he spent all his free nights with Clara, keeping the apartment the government billeted him in for the nights he worked late.

A reminder beeped on his phone: Four o'clock. He straightened his tie and turned back to the towers. Sergeant Harris walked to the entrance from the cafeteria. The sweat glistened on his dark, brown skin, but the faint shades of gray lining the rim of his cap were cool and as straight as the seams on his shirt.

"Sergeant."

"Yes, sir."

"Find Lieutenant Davis and Sergeant Granton. I want you both in my office in half an hour."

"Yes, sir."

*****

It was seven-thirty before the meeting wrapped up. John quickly made his way to the garage and his Indian Chief motorcycle: His great escape. He traveled with it to all his stateside assignments and even his overseas assignments if he was there for more than a few weeks. When he wasn't at work, he was on his motorcycle. He moved toward someplace else — anyplace other than where he was. He liked to take the back roads once past 25th Street. Victory stood there at the inter-section with Broadway where he turned off the main drag. She towered above him and the trees of the boulevard waving her laurel crown in testimony to heroes of the past, inviting viewers to prove their worthi-ness and pass beyond.

When the stoplight turned red, he lifted the visor of his helmet and studied her countenance. Her face was the calm before the storm. She looked both at him and through him, never wavering, ever seeking a victor to crown. He thought it was sad that a vine twisted its way up her massive sword, testifying to the battles not fought for duty or glory or patriotism or faith. *How would she classify his current battle?* The light changed, and he continued his journey.

He planned for a quick meeting. Everyone agreed Keats needed monitoring. It was the diplomatic solution. Time to enhance security anyway. The project was Keats's, but his flagrant arrogance and des-potic demeanor endeared him to few of the people involved with the project. His fellow scientists tolerated him, but only out of respect for his genius. Before the meeting finished, John received word from Command that the schedule was changing. The "package" would arrive within twenty-four hours. That meant reviewing all security measures, inspecting the facilities again, and finally calling his old friend to find out why the schedule changed. At least Keats would leave for Los Angeles in a few hours to oversee the transfer of his project.

John tried not to think of the project as he dodged the mounting number of tourists puttering along the Seawall. He tried to forget the package and the consequences if he failed to secure it. *Death or worse?* He set the security protocols; no need to review them again. Still, nothing was ever absolutely secure. His military career had not prepared him for this assignment. Nothing could have. He told himself not to worry tonight. *Why had the transfer been moved up?* He would call Colonel Dietrich in the morning to find out what he could. They had gone to West Point together and remained friends. He was almost as thorough as John. Tonight, he reminded himself, held no responsibilities.

It took almost forty-five minutes to reach the house. The number of tourists on the beachfront increased as the days of summer lingered longer and longer. Clara said tourist traffic was the only disagreeable part to living on the west end of the island. She never mentioned hurricanes. Ike had done its damage to Galveston, but Avery's tall house on stilts had withstood the storm surge and winds. He pulled up to the house and saw the three pickups and the VW van that carried various members of Clara's family. There were three Harley motorcycles parked at the house, too. He studied them for a moment then he remembered that Clara's brother, Jacob, was due back from Louisiana today. Tonight, they celebrated his return from that state's penal system.

Before John could remove his helmet, Paw Paw Joe yelled, "Hey, Colonel! I was thinkin' maybe you wouldn't be able to make it tonight."

Huge mounds of crawfish were piled on the picnic table. Grandchildren climbed over Paw Paw's large, round self.

Paw Paw wiped his yellow fingers on his pants and motioned John to join them. "It's good stuff. Jacob brought it in fresh from Loosiana."

"Uncle Jacob was in jail," giggled one of the grandchildren.

"He was takin' a vacation," retorted Maw Maw. "You better go on up and change, John. I don't want you gettin' anythin' on your pretty clothes. Clara's in the kitchen."

John waved at Clara's brothers and their friends standing around the crawfish boiler on the beach. Under the house her sisters-in-law balanced food and children. After three turns of stairs, he arrived on the main living level. The south wall of the house, all windows, filled the house with the last light of day as the sun set over the Gulf. A large deck extended the living area toward the open water. The doors opened to the gulf breeze, which flooded the house. He took in the view, breathing in the salty air. The sky slowly darkened, and the colors of the night transformed the scene with every minute. Far on the horizon, rain clouds mixed with the light to color the sky, arranging the reds and yellows of evening into ever-deepening shades of night. The breeze soothed his head, cooling the stale, muggy air of the afternoon. *Perhaps it was worth the commute time to live out here on the beach.*

"Hey, sweetheart, glad you made it."

Clara walked past him with a tray full of hot rolls, butter, and honey. Though she stood on her toes, he still had to bend low to kiss her. She never asked about his work, but the disappointment on her face at his lateness was evident.

"Something came up."

"We're just getting started. Come on down when you've changed. You ever had crawfish? Ooooh, sweetheart, you don't *know* what you're missing! Avery, don't forget to take your blood pill," she said over her shoulder. "You didn't take it this morning. I saw you walk right past it and your breakfast. If you make yourself sick, don't come looking to me to take care of you."

She continued down the stairs without waiting for an answer.

"Never known her to wait for any man."

John had not noticed Avery in the kitchen. She was arranging a platter with hot dogs.

"Avery! These child'en are gettin' hungry," shouted Maw Maw from below.

"Coming!" she yelled back. "Made hot dogs for the little ones. They think crawfish look too much like roaches. I can set one or two of these aside if you're not feeling very adventurous."

She gave him her mischievous smile and took the platter down the stairs. He was becoming part of this family, and it pleased him.

*****

Captain Christian Black whistled as he walked down to the parking lot of the hotel. The hotel opened to Seawall Boulevard, giving him a view of the Gulf of Mexico from his window. Of all the places to be billeted, this was one of the nicest. He stopped once to tuck his iPad into the outside pocket of his small briefcase and pull out the keys to the rental car. As he reached the car, conveniently parked near the street, he waved at Lieutenant David Davis as he jogged his way into the parking lot.

"DD! What's up? Why are you out running at this ungodly hour of the morning?"

"Morning, Capt'n." Davis was always glad to talk to anyone who wanted to talk, and Captain Black more often than other officers understood Davis. "Don't want to get soft and flabby."

"You say it like it's a bad thing," laughed Black. "Six months and I'm a full-time civilian. It's about time I started filling out. The wife says nobody trusts an accountant who looks too fit. 'Powerful men,' she says, 'are always chubby because they can afford to be.' Never a good thing to argue with the wife."

He patted his enlarging stomach.

"You'll regret it. Once you put the weight on, it doesn't want to come off. Before the army, I was a good fifty pounds heavier. Now, I'm in good shape. And if you haven't noticed, this island is full of skinny little asses just looking for a good-looking man in a uniform."

Davis jokingly flexed his right biceps.

"Hooah!" joked Black. "But still doesn't explain why you're out here so early. Heard Sergeant Gaskin saying he runs PT with his men around dawn. Why not go with them?"

"Colonel doesn't like it. Says I need to set the example. Besides, he says too many of those bikinis I was looking at were jailbait. And I'll be damned if he's not right. Just lost the butter bars, so probably best to listen and concentrate on keeping the silver bar. Besides, with things heating up, our schedules will be hell. Getting in the PT while I can."

"That's what I hate about these assignments. Messes up my routine. I'll warn you now; I'm a bear when my sleep schedule is messed up."

Young David Davis always impressed Black. He had the makings of a good officer, and with his mind for details, he'd be a good fit at the accounting firm where he would start working in January. He'd put the idea in Davis's mind soon to start thinking about his future.

"You be a bear, sir. But I'll outrun you and stay out of the way."

Davis laughed and jogged up the stairs to his room. Captain Black laughed and got in the car. The plane to LA left soon, and he still needed to pick up Dr. Keats.

*****

As he sat under Avery's house that night, John learned to eat crawfish. The Lucas family had welcomed John as they welcomed anyone who wanted family. They drank beer, hard cider, and sweet fruit juice. They laughed at the grandchildren running after the crawfish Uncle Jacob let escape from the bag. After they ate all the crawfish they cleared the dishes, and John walked with Clara on the beach while Paw Paw told ghost stories to the grandchildren. When their mothers said, "Enough," Jacob turned on the radio and danced with his sisters-in-law.

John and Clara danced on the sand, on the other side of the dunes where no one watched them. They would have stayed secluded, but Jacob wanted to dance with his sister the way they had when they were children. They two-stepped to Cajun music then Jacob called for Avery. The two waltzed down the boardwalk leading to the water. Jacob was a big man, a little clumsy, but sincere in his dance. His beer belly and crew cut contrasted with Avery's sleek silhouette. Avery enjoyed the dance and flowed like an actress in an old movie. Finally, Paw Paw said it was time for bed. The children were getting crabby and the rain would land soon. John and Clara sat a while longer on the beach under the stars as a tanker moved toward the coast.

Shortly after one in the morning, he woke. The front door opened and closed. The lock clicked. Clara lay still, deep in sleep. He listened. Just under the sound of the waves and the wind, just under the creaking of the curtain rings shifting in the breeze, soft footsteps walked across the boardwalk to the beach. By now he knew Avery's custom of taking late night walks, but it bothered him knowing she was out wandering the beaches by herself late at night. Whenever he voiced concern for her safety, she would shrug and say, "Who says I'm alone? Besides, can anyone really be alone on an island inhabited by over fifty thousand people?"

"You should be careful," he insisted.

She would simply smile, say "Thanks," and go on her way.

On most nights he woke up when she went out and quickly fell back to sleep. Tonight, he did not. He was always tense before a new assignment, but this time was different. Tomorrow night, the package would be here. As much as he'd tried to forget the job, it hounded his thoughts. The whole thing was wrong. The package shouldn't exist. That was the problem. Nothing had prepared him for this assignment or for finding a family he cared so much for. He slid out of the bed without waking Clara and stepped out of the open door to the deck where the sea breeze brushed his body. The clouds were translucent. A delicate mist flowed down from the sky on the breeze. It would pass in a moment. He let it cover him and cool him. The moon, distant and waning, shed a faint blue light through the wispy clouds. The blue light glided along the water until the water turned black and mixed with the sky. Avery stood, a tiny figure against the dark blue Gulf. She stood as in a painting near the surf line. *Watching or waiting?*

A buzzing noise stirred his attention away from Avery. That made tonight different. The sound was familiar—motorcycles. The sound didn't come from behind him on the road; it came from the beach, far to the west. Avery remained standing, staring at the dark waters of the Gulf, her hair flowing on the wind.

He saw them—at least a dozen motorcycles racing down the beach. He heard yelling over the engines as they drew closer. They were heading straight for Avery. She turned her head to face them. She must see them. He started to call out, but suddenly they drove past her, except for one. The other riders stopped further down the beach, but one rider stopped next to her. John held his breath, deciding what to do.

The driver dismounted the bike. He was a tall silhouette, strong arms, muscular chest. They started talking.

John hurried to the gate on the opposite side of the balcony. Locked. Before he jumped the fence to the stairs, Avery reached up, pushing the man's hair out of his face. He remounted his bike. All the engines revved. Avery walked around the bike, putting her hands around the driver and mounting the bike behind him. They sped away. The other bikers waited for them and then followed.

John stood for a moment, heart pounding as he listened to the sound of the bikes fading away.

"Jacob," he said to no one. "He and Avery danced together."

He allowed himself to relax and returned to the bedroom.

He slid himself between the sheets. Only then did he notice Clara's eyes, wide and glistening, staring at him from beneath strands of hair. He pushed the hair out of her face. She smiled.

"Sorry," he said, "didn't mean to wake you."

She stroked his face. "You're wet, silly. Avery will be fine. She always is."

"It's not safe." He didn't say anything else.

She continued to stroke his face, wiping away the faint layer of rain. He took her hand and kissed it. His body tensed as he stared at her. His heart beat faster.

Clara pulled him to her. "As long as we're both awake..."

He placed his lips on hers, letting the tension swell as he pressed himself against her. She responded by pushing her own body onto his, leaving no space between them. She let out a long sigh as their lips separated, and he kissed her jawline and then her neck. She rubbed her hands along his chest and thighs.

It was late. They were both tired, but they loved the feel of each other's body, and they loved to love.

2

Somewhere in the night, under a hazy moon, beneath a blanket of mist, beyond the lights of the streets, on a bed of sand sits a dog on the watch. Pricked ears tune in on what no human can hear. An old man's shoes lie near the dog. It's quiet, except for the wind, and the surf, and the cracking gulls, and a radio fading into silence as the batteries die as it sits in the sand lying near the old man's shoes and the waiting dog.

Who yearns for the rosy kiss that breaks the night?
Not I, your host in this nocturnal pantheon.
For dawn bids me say adieu,
And all my children to their beds proceed.
Well, most of them.
I'm Mary Midnight. You're listening to KMND Galveston.
The day comes and I must go.
The night may give you dreams that chill
but the light will shatter your illusions.

John woke at five, as he did every morning. He wasn't the kind to lie in bed when awake, but this morning he lay listening to Clara's soft breath as it flowed in and out with the sound of the surf. The sound comforted his fears. The breeze wrapped around them, brushing his face with the lacy curtains from the windows. He stroked her left cheek. She sighed. He smiled and got out of bed.

John's five o'clock routine was silent. He picked up his running clothes from the top of the dresser, the sweatband from the bathroom, his socks from the dryer, a glass of juice from the kitchen, and his running shoes by the door. On the picnic table where he learned to eat crawfish, he tied his shoes. Running on the beach in the early morning provided him with peace of mind and a clear head: the constant thudding surf, the rustling grass, and the calls of gulls were like the rising sun, renewing. *I could get used to this.* Before starting his run, he turned to scan the boardwalk and the house. The French doors on the deck leading to Avery's bedroom swung back and forth with the breeze. The curtains flapped in and out. He wondered if she made it home.

This morning he missed the solace his runs offered him. The sweat dripping down his back tingled, but offered no relief from the heat his body generated. The surf kept pace as he ran, each wave rolling in a little closer. He continued running, his eyes straining into the predawn shadows. The first rays of rose began to beam over the horizon, and a sliver of moon still lit the sand and sea. A seagull dove at a large piece of driftwood near the dunes to his left. It squawked then fought the breeze to regain altitude.

As he neared his turnaround point, he noticed a car parked near the water's edge. The waves splashed the front tires. *Stupid,* he sighed, *tide's going to strand him.*

He paused. A movement in the dunes caught his attention. That was when he felt that tightening he got in the pit of his stomach when something was wrong. John had worked too many missions not to pay attention to that feeling. He peered into the long shadows. While the dawning sun provided enough light for running, it darkened the shadows. He slowly walked toward the dunes. A cool breeze washed across his face; then the gulf winds picked up behind him. *Laughing?* A man's almost silent laugh. It was faint, distant, moving away in the wind. *Is that a radio?* His skin crawled. The radio hissed and then stopped making any noise. A pair of old, tired sneakers sat beside it. Before he reached the vegetation line, a dog barked, and a young, red-headed fisherman walked out from behind the dunes pulling up his waders and trying to shake off the mongrel intent on following him.

"Morning," he said.

"Morning," said John.

The glow of dawn chased out the shadows. *It's the job. This time it's getting to me.*

"Guess I'd better move my car."

"Good idea."

John's jog back to the house took longer than usual. He felt nervous, continually turning his head to look behind him, but saw nothing more than the shape of the dog sitting on the dunes watching the fisherman. At the boardwalk, he stopped and stretched. Avery's house was one among a small cluster of houses. Each house was close enough to be seen, but far enough away from the other for the illusion of privacy. He noticed the door to Avery's room was closed, and the curtains were drawn tight. The lights were on upstairs in the living room. Clara sat in the easy chair next to the window with the newspaper opened wide. The thought of coffee filled his head. She wouldn't expect him to greet her until he showered and dressed.

"Good run this morning?" Clara asked as she bounced from sink to stove to counter reigning over her kitchen. John watched for a moment in odd speculation at her sudden, jerky gyrations until he moved closer to the kitchen and realized the radio was playing. Just above a whisper, REM's *It's the End of the World As We Know It was* coming from the small docking station in the kitchen. John could not imagine Clara being still.

"Good. Sleep well?"

He picked up his tablet, opened it to the news, and sat at the table. No one went into the kitchen when Clara was cooking.

"Like a baby. I've opened a can of chili. Want eggs with it?"

"Two, please. Hear anything this morning?" John asked as he scanned the local news.

"Just the wind and surf. Why?" Clara did not lose a beat as she cracked an egg open on the side of the skillet.

"Thought I heard something while I was running."

"Probably some drunk tourist passed out on the beach. Beach Patrol will find him soon enough and take care of him."

John looked at her. She was the soul of compassion with her animals and to the people who mattered, but mention tourists and she was immune to any distress they might have. Since arriving in Galveston, he daily witnessed the ambivalence the natives showed to their visitors.

"Most likely."

He wished more than believed Clara's explanation.

Clara stopped moving to gaze hard into his face. "Something wrong?"

"No. Seems hotter today than yesterday. Want to have lunch? I'm working tonight."

"Sure. Should be through with surgery by noon. Light load this morning, a teeth cleaning and a couple of neuters. I won't start seeing patients till after three, but afraid to tell you, sweetie, it's only June. It's going to get hotter."

John grimaced. "At least the air conditioning works. We'll have a nice long lunch at home today." His expression changed to a wide grin, and he winked at her.

Clara returned his grin. "Your eggs are done. Come fix your plate."

Avery came up the stairs and slunk into the kitchen. "Y'all have to have the radio on so damn loud first thing in the morning?"

She opened the refrigerator then stepped back squinting at the light.

"I made chili and eggs," said Clara.

Avery picked up the pan of chili sitting on the stove. She curled up her nose and set it back on the stove. "Didn't you set a package of hamburger out yesterday?"

"Top shelf. I stashed it up there when Mama called to say Jacob was coming in with the crawfish. You like chili and eggs." Clara stopped filling a bowl with chili, made a puzzled expression and dumped the contents of the bowl back into the pot of chili.

Avery pulled out some meat and slapped it between her hands to make a patty. "Not this morning. Are you making toast?"

"Nope. We're out of bread. I'll add it to the list." Clara was pouring Fritos onto her chili. "Where did you put the list anyway?"

"You told me you put it on the desk. Be sure you have it when we got to the store tonight. I'm not coming back here just for that." With obviously little thought, she grabbed a large skillet from the counter and set it on the stove.

"You told me you quit yesterday," said John.

"I do have other things to do than deal with your group. Besides, Jerk-off won't be there. He's picking up your precious little package and won't be back till I'm out of there." She tossed the patty into the skillet. It sizzled.

John halted the cup of coffee on its way to his lips. He wondered what she knew about the package. Clara sat beside him and stirred together her chili, chips, and eggs.

"Oh, chill, John," said Avery smirking at his irritated expression as she flipped over the hamburger patty.

"It's a little hard, sweetheart," started Clara, "for her not to have some idea of what's going on. She coordinates your activities with the school. She's not out to steal State secrets. Pick me up from the office, will you Avery? John and I are having lunch, so I'll let him take me back to the office. You won't have to drive all the way here first."

John decided it was better to laugh it off than continue the conversation. He changed the subject. Avery placed the patty on a plate and sat down at the table.

"Are you going to eat that? It's not cooked yet."

"I cooked it."

"It's still bleeding."

"That's the way you're supposed to eat red meat. That's why they label it *red*. Clara, can you reach the corn chips on the counter behind you, please?"

"Red meat is good for the blood," said Clara. "You're awfully pale. You okay?"

"This form of pallor is called a hangover."

"Okay but take an extra iron this morning, you look like the walking dead."

"Yes, mother."

Avery grabbed more chips. John watched the two of them over his bowl of chili. He believed, with reservation, that Avery didn't know about the package. He hoped that Clara didn't.

*****

"How you want to handle it?" asked Sergeant Emmanuel Granton. He and Sergeant Vincent Harris sat at a corner table in the cafeteria far away from the few others eating in the pre-dawn hours.

Harris continued slicing through the yolks of his eggs without seeing them. "Nothing's for certain, but the death stirred up the Generals and made them move up the schedule. We need to make sure we're saying the same thing. Espinoza wants only facts, no speculation, but rumors run on their own. Only so much we can control."

"Celia didn't buy the mugging story," said Granton. "But she didn't ask any questions."

"You talked to her already? I only met her once. Good looking woman with a good head on her shoulders. Seemed like a good master sergeant's wife."

"Sure is," began Granton, but then he corrected himself. "Was."

"Not a lot of folks liked him?"

"He was good at his job, but he could be..." Granton nibbled some toast and thought about his words. "A bit 'in your face,' if you know what I mean. Always working even when he was off duty."

"Gotch' you." Harris patted his chin with his napkin, folded it, and placed it next to his plate. "I heard he could handle that Keats fellow. We could sure use Haskins here for that. Oh, well. A good trooper is down, God rest. We can only hope the others turn up somewhere, but..." He didn't finish his sentence.

Granton crossed himself and repeated, "God rest. We have a lot of work to do."

"Exactly. Stick to the facts. Just deliver them the way that makes sense. Found dead on the beach. Local police say he was jumped by a gang while out searching for some wayward troopers. We say we're taking nothing the local cop says for granted. We'll wait for our own folks to tell us what happened. I don't want anyone questioning where his Troops are. We got it covered. Nothing to affect anybody here."

"He was mean enough for his own troops to turn on him. That's what some folks will say. Maybe we shouldn't discourage that kind of talk." Granton contemplated his coffee before continuing. Harris had worked with Espinoza for a lot of years. "Colonel thinks they're dead, doesn't he?"

"Oh, yeah. And he's pissed. I've worked with him too long not to see the signs. He gets extra quiet, cool like, and mutters to himself until he figures out what to do." Harris plunged his toast into the egg yolks and began to eat again. "He'll get us through this. Don't you worry about that." He began to chuckle. "Although, that woman he's hanging out with does seem to be cooling his heels a bit. Never thought I'd see that."

Granton laughed. "You married men always looking for that angle, aren't you? Like a woman is going to change a man."

"You wait, Manny. You'll get yourself hooked up one day."

They sat for a while in silence eating their breakfast. Neither wanted to admit it, but the death hung over their heads. As experienced soldiers, they ate their meal, but they didn't taste it. They made small talk, but they didn't pay attention to what they said. They planned, prepared for what might come.

"Here you are, gentlemen." A woman in a cafeteria uniform walked up with two large cups to go. "Coffee to go. You look like you need it, and I just made a fresh pot. I see your folks gathering for PT, but plenty of time before that to fuel up. And don't you go reaching for your wallets. On the house. Enjoy."

She walked away.

Each sergeant smiled and picked up their trays and coffee. Keep moving forward; a job needed doing, and they would see it was done.

"Seeing as how you're the senior, I'll give you the honors." Granton smiled sheepishly.

"No sweat. Figured as much." As they walked out, the first rays of the sun crested over the buildings and shadows began to slide away. "So, how well you know Celia?"

*****

Keats hated flying as military cargo. Instead of leaning back in a first-class seat, enjoying a glass of wine and fine music, he suffered the smell of sweat and grease on a hard seat while bouncing up and down next to common soldiers. *Certainly, the project requires the highest security, but this is absurd.* He would complain to Colonel Dietrich, who knew how important Keats was to the project. This Espinoza needed things explained to him.

"Is it really necessary to rush around like this? Why the sudden change in schedule? I already had my flight booked," he shouted to Capt. Black, Espinoza's administrative officer.

"Most efficient means, Dr. Keats." Capt. Black looked up from the book he was reading on his tablet. Its light cast hard shadows on a puffy face verging on chubby and small, graceless eyes. "But don't worry. I'll be able to get a full refund for your booking, what with this being a military operation."

With six months until retirement, and a position in his father-in-law's accounting firm awaiting him, he could take with ease whatever task the army assigned him. Even this one, which admittedly still sounded preposterous, but if Colonel Espinoza and the others took it seriously, so would he, at least for six more months.

"I wasn't worried about that." Keats expected to get more from the overly efficient administrator. He might be an accountant, but his strictly logical mannerisms made it impossible for him to hide information. "Any idea why we're doing this now instead of next week as planned?"

Captain Black had already turned back to his book. The latest theory on forensic accounting was fascinating. "Afraid I'm not privy to that information, sir. I'm strictly a numbers man. Colonel Espinoza only sent me as a favor, as one of my girls just had her tonsils out. Everything went well, but she could do with a visit from Daddy. You know what I mean. I'm sure Colonel Dietrich will have the particulars you need. I'll be joining you for the flight back."

Keats raged inside. A babysitter? *That son-of-a-bitch Espinoza sent a babysitter with me! Who the hell does he think he is?*

"Are you all right, sir? You look a little red. There are some airsick bags under the seat. Would you like me to call the medic?"

"I'm fine."

There were times when Keats hated the army for funding his project.

Captain Black returned to his book.

*****

Her last patient came in at seven thirty. It was Bela, an eight-year-old mutt the size of a small child. It was time for his annual check-up and shots. He was a sweetheart of a dog unless you were not one of the few people whom he liked. It didn't matter that his overprotective owner kept him at her heel, people were afraid of him or thought he was too cute. The first group he got along well with, he snarled at the latter. Oblivious to his behavior, the owner worried more about her dog getting a shot than the humans around her.

"Well, hey, Bela," Clara said. "How you doin'?"

Bela uttered that faint growl of recognition as Clara knelt to his eye level and extended her hand to him in the exam room. He didn't snip at her. Her hand held a treat, dried liver. His eyes focused on the treat, then at his owner, then he sniffed the liver in the extended hand.

"Come on, Bela. It's yummy. How are things going with him?" Clara asked.

"No problems."

Bela took the treat as his owner tried to smile through trembling lips.

"Good boy!" said Clara.

Bela let her pet him.

"If you've got food, you're a friend," the owner laughed.

That friendship, however, lasted until the owner placed the muzzle over his snout, the tech wrapped him in his arms, and Clara began the exam. Then he'd shake and whine.

Clara examined cats, dogs, birds, snakes, and every kind of pet brought into her office or that she could visit. She even oversaw the care of several of the island's small herds of cattle and the horses for the special needs kids at Hope Arena. But when the big, gruff dogs such as Bela whined as she brought out a needle, Clara always felt a twinge of sympathetic pain. Some animals took the needle without noticing. Most squirmed, spat, and twisted to get away from her, but Bela's cry pierced her heart. She couldn't decide what tugged at her heart the most — the sound itself or those big, round, brown eyes welling up with tears.

As soon as the exam and shots were over, Bela wagged his tail and followed his owner out the front door. He was never sick, and the owner always paid cash.

The workday over, Clara sat at her desk, staring at the pile of paperwork that included surgery notes, test results, exam notes, bills, staff schedules, and payroll. She sorted through the papers and picked out those that needed her attention the most. As she sorted, she thought again about the value of a secretary.

"It's not like the business can't afford it," she told the walls of her office. "I said I'd get one before and I didn't, but this time it's different; I really need a secretary. Maybe just part time. That wouldn't cost too much."

She continued debating the issue to no one.

"Dr. Lucas!" Miguel, Clara's assistant, yelled from the hallway. "We've cleaned up back here. You want me to lock up?"

Clara leaned out the door scratching her head. "Go ahead. I'll turn the alarm on when I leave."

"All right. I've forwarded the phones already." Miguel stopped, glanced at her and noted the paperwork on her desk. "You should really get a secretary."

"Thanks, Miguel. Good night."

Clara rolled her eyes into her head when she realized that the door to her office had, as usual, been open and that he'd listened to her debate with herself.

"Do I ever not talk out loud?" she asked no one in particular.

Clara liked this time of the day in her office. She liked checking on the animals recovering from surgery and the animals left by their owners afraid of leaving their beloved pets in ordinary kennels.

"So, if I get a secretary will it really save me any time with the paperwork?" she confided to a black cat with a bandage around its paw. Clara checked the bandage then closed the door to the cat's kennel. "I'd probably just have to do it all myself, anyway. I mean, you know, it's not like she's going to know how I like things done. I'd spend all my time telling her what to do."

She moved over to a small dog that woke from its sleep at the sound of her voice and yawned from deep inside the dreaded cone. Clara opened the kennel door to scratch the dog's ears.

"Sorry. You're right. A secretary could be a he, but I'm sure I'd still have to spend all my time doing everything."

With everything in place, she turned off the lights to the kennel room and started down the hall to the front. As she passed the storeroom something thudded to the floor. She froze and listened. It was quiet except for the animals stirring in their cages. She listened until her heart slowed to its normal speed. She opened the storeroom and found Muffin, the office cat, meandering along the upper shelf. A can of horse ointment lay on the floor.

"What are you doing in here?"

Muffin leapt softly into Clara's arms and nuzzled under her chin purring.

"You're in so much trouble for spooking me like that. I ought to throw you out on the street."

Muffin ignored her and purred while nuzzling Clara's chin.

"Hey, where's Gaston? Gaston!" He usually made rounds with her.

Gaston, like Muffin, was an office pet, a brown and white mutt Clara rescued one day on the Seawall. He had a large scar that started on his snout, traced his eye and ended where his left ear should have been. It gave him a strangely tuff-guy but at the same time homely look. He had lived in the office for so long she put his name on the office door. Underneath *Clara Lucas, D.V.M.* was *Gaston, D.O.G.*

Clara walked back to the kennel room with Muffin in her arms. Gaston sat in front of the cages, back straight, ear poised for optimal listening. Gaston stared past Clara and Muffin. He made that little growl dogs make when they are unsure of a threat.

"Gaston, what's the matter with you?"

He growled louder. Muffin yowled and jumped out of Clara's arms, scratching her forearm.

"Muffin!" she exclaimed.

"Are you going to keep me waiting all night?"

Clara jumped at the sound of Avery's voice.

Avery stood silhouetted in the hall, hands on her hips. Gaston barked a warning. Clara turned back to the dog to reprimand him, but Avery spoke first.

"That's enough, Gaston."

Her voice was quiet and smooth. Gaston lay down, resting his snout on his forepaws. His eyes remained on Avery.

"What's wrong with you?" asked Clara. She bent down and scratched where his lost ear should be. "You doing okay? Let me see your eyes."

"Seriously? He's a dog. He's doing what dogs do. Let's go. It stinks back here."

Avery didn't wait for an answer. She turned and headed toward the front. Before Clara followed, she noted how quiet the kennel room was. Muffin watched Avery from under a stool draped with an old towel. Clara made a mental note to inspect the kennels the next day.

Thursday night was grocery night. It was long established as the one night they were too tired to do much else. If they didn't schedule a night, it wouldn't get done. Living on the west end of the island meant it was impossible to make a quick run to the grocery store, and in the summer the stores were too full of tourist for a quick trip anywhere.

Avery waited in the car for Clara to turn out the lights and set the alarm. On most Thursdays, she met Avery at home, but this afternoon John had driven her to the office on his way back to work. Until tonight Clara had never thought to wonder why Avery didn't come to the office anymore.

"How did you get into the office?" she asked as she climbed into the passenger seat of Avery's jeep.

"I opened the door and walked in."

"Miguel said he was going to lock the door."

"He forgot. Sue him. You got the list?"

Avery turned the key to start the car. She wanted to laugh when she asked but held back. They always forgot the list.

"You said you had it."

"Why would I have it? You said this morning it was on the desk."

"No, you said I said I knew where it was. I just said we needed to add bread."

Clara buckled her seat belt.

"Well, I didn't have it when I left the house." Avery backed out of the parking space. "I bet John moved it to aggravate me."

"Since he's not here, he's as good a person to blame as anyone else. It's not like we need it. Do we?"

"I have no intention of driving back to the house for it."

Avery pulled out of the parking lot and headed east on Seawall Boulevard. They tried every week to get organized, and every week failed. At least they always had a good excuse for not having it.

Clara leaned back letting the wind blow through her hair and cool her head. The sun danced with the water, sending its last rays of color on the blue, fading sky. There were enough cars on Seawall Boulevard to slow the drive. Tomorrow the traffic would be intolerable. She leaned back and listened to the seagulls squawking in the air and the water splashing on the rocks.

At a red light, Clara turned to Avery, "Why don't you ever come to my office anymore?"

"It stinks."

Avery turned her head to check the traffic before shifting the jeep into gear.

"You used to like to help out."

"Things change."

"It couldn't be John's project, could it? The army only came to town at the start of summer."

"If I told you, John would have to kill you." The corners of Avery's mouth turned up into a grin. She concluded the discussion. Whatever Avery was up to, she wasn't sharing tonight. "Looks like we're in for a good crowd this weekend."

*****

The facilities at Los Angeles Air Force Base were superior to the facilities in Galveston. The University in Galveston had good labs, but Keats had not built them from scratch as he had here. Everything was familiar and comfortable.

Captain Black left him as soon as the plane landed. Colonel Dietrich met him as he logged into the lab building. The first thing Keats noticed was the number of guards. Their numbers and the weapons they openly carried indicated that something had happened. Dietrich's normally pale complexion had greyed around the edges. Bags hung under his eyes. Even his voice sounded weary.

"Good to see you again, Doctor. Hope you had an easy flight."

"Hardly. You might be used to cargo planes, but my ass is bruised in places I didn't know existed, I'm starving, and I need a drink. What's wrong with my boy? That's the only reason I can think of for such an abrupt change in a schedule."

Dietrich hesitated to speak as they made their way through the security doors and walked toward Keats's office and lab. "Hang on," said Keats. "Let's get to my office. Unless Cross has taken over my office, there should be a bottle of whiskey in my desk. Looks like we could both use a drink."

The door to Keats's office opened to a paneled room with windows facing west. He pulled out his phone, tapped, and lights glowed and window blinds opened. He tossed his satchel on a leather couch, reached for a drawer on his desk and pulled out a half-full bottle of whiskey. Colonel Dietrich pulled two glasses from the bar shelf and took them to the desk. He watched as Keats poured.

"So, what the hell is going on? Why wasn't I consulted on the change of plans?"

Colonel Dietrich drank his whiskey with one gulp. Keats reached to pour him another, but Dietrich stopped him. "I better keep my wits about me."

Keats sipped his drink and waited patiently for Colonel Dietrich to tell him what he needed to know.

"You remember Sergeant Haskins? He worked with you and Cross to bring in the boy. Helped Cross find him in that youth shelter."

"Yes." Sergeant Haskins was one of the few non-commissioned officers Keats worked well with. "Intelligent and well educated. I like him. A good liaison and an efficient man to work with."

"He's dead, missing two days along with three of his troops. They were checking the places the boy talked about to see what they could find out about the 'others.' They didn't come back." Dietrich paused, allowing Keats to consider the possibilities. "Local police found Haskins's body yesterday washed up on a nearby beach. Still no sign of his unit."

"You've done an autopsy?"

"Your people wanted you to oversee it."

"Working hypothesis as to cause of death?"

"None, but they tell me there is not a drop of blood in him."

Keats finished his drink and poured another. "I'll eat, then get to work. I don't see why the project needs to be moved. The security here is excellent, Sergeant Haskins's demise aside. You've seen to that. You should have consulted me before deciding anything."

Dietrich breathed deeply. He didn't like working with civilians. They questioned too much when the answers should be obvious.

"Can't take chances on these *others* finding their way in here. Espinoza is the better security man for this job, and the island is smaller, an easier area to control."

"I thought you were the expert on security. Obviously, things are moving forward, so I'll take your word for Colonel Espinoza's abilities." Keats didn't like the answer, but with the army funding the research, it was pointless to argue. "Join me for dinner? I think I'll order from the surf-and-turf place just off the base."

"Thanks, but I better get back to work."

Dietrich returned to his own office. He liked the institutional gray walls and metallic desk. It was comfortable for a career man like himself. He switched on the monitor to his computer and logged into the security cameras. In Keats's lab the boy sat across from Charles Cross. The boy was talkative, animated.

"Oh, come on, Charlie. You didn't really, did you?" the boy laughed

"Yes, I did." Cross laughed with the boy.

Dietrich looked at the photo of his family and shuddered. *Something's wrong.*

*****

"That was my last army in South America."

"You're not paying attention. Keep your eyes on the entire board or your enemies sneak in and take what's yours." Cross laughed a little, then started coughing and pulled out his inhaler.

"You should get some rest, Charlie. You look tired. And if we have to move tomorrow—"

"We *are* moving. Don't think we won't. I told you about Sergeant Haskins." Cross lowered his voice. They were alone in the room, but someone was always watching and listening. The discovery of Haskins's body had put everyone on edge. The guards glared at Jason when they saw him even though he had been in custody for nearly three weeks. "Everyone is worried."

"He never liked me," snapped Jason, letting his anger roll out of his mouth without caution.

"Jason." Cross picked up Jason's hand. He suddenly pulled his hand back remembering the cameras. "A man is dead. Those he was with might also be dead. You had nothing to do with it, but you should still show a little consideration for those they left behind."

"You're right. I'm sorry." Jason held his head low, but the venom of his voice continued, if only at a low hiss. "If they were looking for the others, Tomás would have found out. They'll all be dead by now. Or worse."

"Tell me more about Tomás?"

Jason said nothing, continuing to stare at the floor.

"Jason, I can't help you if you're not honest with me and tell me everything."

"I told you before. I met him about the same time I met you, back when you were out recruiting people to be part of your study. It was getting cold out at night. You found me in the doorway to the Chinese restaurant, said I could earn seventy-five dollars just for giving a blood sample and answering a few questions. I thought I had it made, especially when you said I could earn more if I helped you bring others in for the test. I thought you were another perv. But you were nice to me, bought me a chicken dish from the Chinese place, the one with all the peppers on it. Remember how the peppers popped in your mouth? And then you got me that leather-like jacket, the ones with the chains hanging on it. Who would have thought we'd end up here?"

Cross walked around the room. He wanted to hug Jason, tell him everything would be okay, let him understand that he had a friend, but the cameras were always on. He settled for patting Jason on the back.

"It was a few nights later that I found Tomás, or maybe he found me. He knew all about me. How did he know when you didn't, Charlie?

You didn't even know I was weird until you found me almost two weeks later."

Jason's breath began to shorten. His green eyes gleaned with that look of panic Cross had seen before, like when he told Jason about the death of Sergeant Haskins.

Cross stoked Jason's hair, trying to smooth out its wild, wiry curls. "It's going to be okay, Jason."

"But he's just like me or like I will be. They all were. I'm not alone, a freak, Charlie." Panic oozed out of each word. "They said they were my friends, but they weren't. They wanted me dead, just like that sergeant who died, just like all these people here. Charlie, I don't want to die."

Jason's eyes pleaded for help. He shook, and tears rolled down his face falling onto the Risk board.

"We're going to find out what's wrong with you. Dr. Keats will be here in a few hours. I promise; we're going to figure this out. You have a disease or a condition or something."

"Ouch!" Jason jerked his head to the side. "Stop pulling out my hair."

Cross jumped back, realizing his school ring had caught onto some of Jason's hair and pulled. "I'm so sorry, Jason. I didn't mean..."

It broke the tension in Jason, and he began to laugh. Cross smiled.

"If you can't cure me, at least make it a quick end. Don't pull my hair out one piece at a time."

Cross pulled fine red hairs from his ring but stopped laughing. "It won't be like that, Jason. I promise. We're going to find a cure. Dr. Keats and I have already made remarkable progress. I'm almost certain that I've found the anomaly in your blood that's making you sick. It won't be long now."

"You keep saying that, and I want to believe you, but I don't believe Keats wants to help me. He's weird. He likes to boss everyone around like he owns the place or something. He looks at me and I don't see someone who wants to help me."

"Milton Keats is a brilliant man. He might be a little hard to take, but that's only because he sees things differently than everybody else. He does want to cure you, but he also sees the potential that this odd disease or mutation in the blood could mean to other people who are ill. Please, Jason, have a little faith. If not in him, in me."

Jason smiled. Cross was always good to him. "Okay. I'll have faith in you as long as I don't have to deal with Keats too often. But, Charlie, watch out for the others. He's scary, although not the scariest one that I saw. We've got to be careful."

"That's why the army's here. They won't let anything get to you." Cross moved back to his chair at the table with the board game. "Come on. Let's finish this game. I'm about to win. And once I do that, we'll get a bit of sleep. It's going to be a long day."

*****

The parking lot at the grocery store was not too crowded but plenty of weekenders came down early, and residents were trying to beat the tourists. There was plenty of parking available, as far from the door as they could get. Inside the store they followed their usual routine: Get what they needed and dodge as many carts pushed by children as possible. Finally, look for Tommy, their new, favorite checker.

Tommy had started working at the store with the other kids when school closed for the summer. He was now Avery and Clara's favorite checker. He was too cute not to be. They decided that he wasn't more than fifteen. He was so small the employee-issued white starched shirt looked as if it were going to swallow him whole. As he scanned their groceries, he chatted constantly, halting every third item to push golden curls off his forehead. What Clara liked best about Tommy was his clear, blue eyes that laughed with affection. Sometimes she thought they were too clear as though he was looking right through her. However, Tommy always smiled happily when Avery and Clara came to his register. She could not help but like him.

Avery went to the floral section to pick out flowers for the table, and Clara headed for register three — Tommy's register. Her eyes were half closed as she envisioned the inside of the refrigerator at home and wondered if they had picked up all they needed. She debated whether or not to go back for more butter as she pushed her cart into Tommy's aisle. Instead of the usual smiling eyes to greet her, she narrowly missed running the cart into a longhaired man in jeans and a black t-shirt leaning over the credit card scanner. Tommy crouched mouse-like behind the counter as though he were in the claws of a cat.

Clara stared for a moment, then asked, "Are you open?" and purposely nudged the cart into the longhaired man.

He turned his head, looking down at her with a large and unfriendly grin.

"Yes ma'am. I'll be right with you." Tommy's voice shook.

The man in the black t-shirt took in Clara with a quick glance. He leaned one arm on the check stand. If he were any taller, his shadow would have engulfed her. He wasn't one of the usual tourists. His wolfish grin, dark hair, and lean body might have been attractive, but the eyes that stared down on Clara pierced her usual armor. They glowed with the reflection of the register lamp. He leaned closer to her. Her instincts told her to step back, but she stayed firm in her spot determined to show no fear. Suddenly, he looked away, smirked, and left the aisle.

"How are you tonight, Ms. Clara, Ms. Avery?"

Tommy recovered faster than Clara. She wasn't sure how long Avery had been standing behind her.

As soon as they left Tommy's register, Clara began a tirade on the longhaired man. "I ... some people ... I mean some people have a lot of nerve." Clara rattled on as she and Avery made their way to the car. "They just think they can go around threatening anyone they please because they're bigger than everybody else."

"Suppose he's just one of those people with a frightening disposition."

"You don't know that," Clara replied irritably.

She stopped and followed Avery's gaze to the other side of the lot. The longhaired man lazily sat on a motorcycle parked under a light pole. Despite the length of the parking lot, Clara was certain that he was looking at them. Perhaps it was a trick of the evening lights, but Clara decided that he was smiling at Avery.

"You know him!" she declared. "I can't believe you've let me go on and on about the SOB, and you haven't said a word!"

"When did you give me a chance?" Avery placed the last bag of groceries in the back seat. "Besides, you're right; he shouldn't have been picking on Tommy in the store. I'm sure it was just a bit of harmless fun, but still, it was very naughty."

The longhaired man laughed and rode away. Clara noticed that he glanced back at Avery. Clara was certain that he had heard their conversation, despite the distance between them.

"So ... why haven't I heard about this guy before now?"

Clara's curiosity of Avery's love life overcame her indignity at being allowed to rant on about the disconcerting episode. A large grin formed despite her intentions to be miffed.

"Not much to say." Avery pulled onto the street. "I go riding with Max and the boys sometimes."

"Just go riding with the boys, huh?" Clara wasn't sure whether she was pleased for her friend. "And I suppose you and Max are just friends."

"Sure." Avery flashed her best sarcastic grin.

"And the sex?"

"Great." Avery started to laugh as she pulled onto Seawall Boulevard. "What? Suddenly you're the only one on the island allowed to get any?"

Clara could only laugh at herself and with Avery. She hadn't seen her friend laugh for a long while.

*****

Avery and Clara made their way west on Seawall Boulevard. Tommy came out of the store on his break. Full night had settled in, but the store and Seawall Boulevard were flooded with lights. He stopped to talk to another clerk taking a smoke on the bench by the door. The smoker told one of his usual bad jokes, but Tommy laughed anyway. He said he wanted to walk around — get some air. He reached the edge of the store next to the alley between the supermarket and the strip center. Noticing an empty box, he picked it up to throw it out. No one parked in front of the dark alley at night. He took a few steps into the alley toward the dumpster when a cat leaped out of the dumpster and ran out into the parking lot. Tommy flinched. "I hate cats," he said.

Tommy threw the box into the dumpster. That was when he saw the shadow that had made the cat run. His cherub face steeled. He lowered his eyes as his shoulders lifted then relaxed.

"Sir," he said with respect and caution.

"It's been a long time, Thomas. The grocery business suits you much better than conquests."

"It suits our purpose."

"Our purpose, Thomas?"

"We have mutual interest on the island. Our kind is in jeopardy. We need to remove the threat before —"

"You were told to stand down." The man's voice neither rose in volume nor increased in speed, but its tone pierced the darkness of the ally and thrust itself into Tommy's heart. His usual pale complexion waxed sheet white. He stared harder at the ground. He opened his mouth to speak, but the voice continued. "But as you are here now, you may serve some useful purpose."

"I am pleased to serve however I may, sir."

"Be at the entrance to the hospital by midnight. Bring one or two others who you trust. Hover near this colonel who has taken charge of our young brother. Let me see you not be seen."

"As you wish. Shall I kill him?"

"That's always been your problem, Thomas. You rush in without knowing your enemy. Observe him. Our enemies can teach us a great deal. Don't dismiss their teachings by always killing them. There will be need to kill before long."

"Yes, sir. I'll go now to prepare."

Jason took a step backward to ease out of the dark alley.

"And Thomas ..."

"Sir?"

"Leave the woman to me."

"Yes, sir."

Once again Tommy began to back out of the dark alley. This time he made it into the light of the grocery store's sign. He lifted his head and looked around him, making sure the man was gone. A snicker formed on his lips. He hated the old man as much as he feared him.

"This time," he whispered out loud. "This time leave the fighting to those who know what they're doing, old man."

3

On the UTMB campus in the parking garage in front of Sealy Towers, on the fifth level under a lamppost beneath the stars, a cigarette lies burning on the ground. On the fourth level, darkness. On the third level, two security guards steam the windows of their patrol car to the rhythm of music on the radio. The hour is late. A car turns into the drive in front of the towers. The beams of its headlights glide up the concrete and brick garage. Within the shadows of the fourth floor, a flicker of something, then more darkness.

Someone's watching.
Night's eyes peer through your thoughts.
Night's winds whisper your secrets.
In the night, time stands still — for a moment.
Do you know what side you're on?
I'm Mary Midnight; you're at KMND Galveston.
Why should you fear?
I'm here.

Captain Amanda Hill took another long sip from the beer bottle.

The cool, refreshing taste made her smile. "The first time I met him, I thought I'd shit my pants."

Everyone began laughing. Sergeant was huge, almost too large for the army, and scared just about everybody who met him the first time — the spitting stereotype of the lean, mean, army sergeant who would rather kick your ass than tell you to come to attention.

"I mean, here I am, this little shit second lieutenant straight out of school, and let's face it, I'm four foot nothing, and here is this giant of a sergeant who would send Louise Gossitt Jr. pissing in his pants, and he's saluting *me*. I wanted to shrink into the sidewalk right then and there. But I saluted him, walked past him as fast as I could, and hoped I never had to see him again. And what do you think happened then? Espinoza assigns him to my unit heading to the sandbox."

Everyone, even Celia, laughed with soul, which was the point of the gathering on the front porch of the Haskinses' house. She had been crying since Colonel Dietrich arrived in the morning to tell her of her husband's death. *A mugging gone very wrong. It was a routine assignment to pick up a drunk soldier, but he was attacked, probably a gang. He fought back, but they outnumbered him. The army would do everything it possibly could to make certain justice was served.* At least he spoke the truth regarding justice. Mandy would make sure of that. She emptied the bottle of beer in one, long gulp. Her heart raced with this shitty assignment.

Celia put her hand on Mandy's knee. That was when Mandy knew that Celia knew that Sergeant wasn't killed in a mugging. "He always said you were a good soldier to work with, even if you were an officer and no bigger than a piss-ant."

The laughing continued. Someone offered Mandy another beer, but she waved it away.

"A damn good man, Celia. I'm proud to have served with him. Never would have made it to captain if he hadn't kept me in line." Mandy felt tears forming in her eyes, but she kept them back. No crying in the army, not for a woman and certainly not in front of her own enlisted men.

Celia's family began to arrive at the house. Her oldest son lived in nearby San Diego. It took time to get the kids out of school, but they were home now. Mandy decided family mattered more now than she did to Celia. No need for her to be there anymore. Besides, it was almost time to go to work.

The California sun began its daily descent. Shadows lengthened, but enough light still shone to comfortably walk down the street toward her car. Soldiers and their families passed her going to and from the Haskinses' home. As she neared her car, she first noticed the hairs on her neck standing at attention. She had been fighting tears and not paid much attention to her surroundings. Tall weeds and mounds of dirt gathered by the neighborhood kids for dirt biking filled the large empty lot at the end of the road where Mandy had parked her car. The sun filled the west side of the lot. Long shadows began chasing each other on the east side.

A jack rabbit leapt from one long shadow, cracking the dried grass and shaping a small cloud of dust and dirt. The rabbit frightened two pigeons from their feeding at the foot of a new mound of dirt. They flapped their wings and took flight with a whoop and scrawl. *What scared the rabbit?* Mandy stared hard into the shadows taking shape. For a moment, she thought that within the shadow of the grass, she saw the shadow of a face. *This is bull shit.* The hairs on her neck relaxed. *Wish I hadn't quit smoking.*

* * * * *

Avery stood on the patio watching the waves wash onto the shore in the moonlight. Clara lay on the couch asleep with papers scattered across her and the floor. The blue light of the television cast specters dancing off the windows and along the patio planks. She relished the warm breeze flowing in her hair. It was after midnight.

"Soon," she whispered to no one.

And as though he had been waiting for her to say it, he was there.

"Hello, Harry," she said.

His presence enveloped her long before she caught the shadow moving in the corner of her vision. She smiled but didn't face him. It was always better not to look at him before he wanted to be seen.

He stood close behind her. Long, cold, white fingers slipped onto her shoulders. She leaned onto his hard, cool body. It sent chills down her spine but not from its coldness. That she knew. She leaned her head back to rest on his chest. His lips kissed her neck. He caressed her face then moved his hand down her throat and finally rested on her heart. Her heart began to race. Her breath left her body and did not return.

"Shh," he whispered into her ear. "Soon. Breathe, my love. Breathe."

He squeezed her just enough. Her head straightened as she took a deep breath in. Her heart slowed down to normal.

"How much longer?" she asked.

"Not long. Are things ready for the extraction?"

"Yes and no. Thomas and Max keep having little spats. They don't like each other."

"Thomas will do as he's told." He lifted her right hand to his lips and kissed her palm. "You're as beautiful as ever. So right for you to wait."

Avery turned to him, watching the blue ghosts from the television dance in his eyes. She wanted to kiss his thin, pale lips, but he put his finger to his lips. She closed her eyes.

"Keep breathing," he said. "Tomorrow, you will breathe no more."

He kissed her lips.

Avery concentrated on breathing. She had to. Her heart pounded in her chest. "He'll be here soon."

"Show me."

Avery turned toward Clara still sleeping on the couch. "She'll be fine, won't she?"

"As long as she knows her place. Now, take me where they will take him."

*****

The scream, high and long, startled Clara awake, scattering the papers she had been working on when she fell asleep. The television went to a commercial.

"Damn it!" she said and pushed herself up from the couch.

The house was dark except for the light of the TV, the small table lamp beside her, and the stars reflecting on the water into her living room. She headed for the kitchen, shaking off the sleep. The clock on the microwave read one in the morning. She searched through the refrigerator for the milk and chocolate. The refrigerator light revealed a kitchen much neater now than when she had sat on the couch to write reports — groceries put away, dishwasher empty, and no dirty dishes in the sink.

She turned on the under counter lights and mixed her chocolate milk. The cool chocolate relaxed her throat. The apples on the counter tempted her, but she decided against eating any.

"I should just go to bed. What was I thinking bringing exam notes home to organize?"

Clara's plans for the evening had been simple: pick up groceries, clean kitchen, organize exam notes, then early to bed. When Avery offered to put the groceries away and tidy the kitchen, Clara jumped at the chance to get ahead with the paperwork. The cake decorating show she liked to watch was coming on. Her plan for a quiet, productive evening without John had seemed to be working out. She didn't know what time she fell asleep. The last thing Clara remembered was channel surfing, notes running together, and Avery bustling in the kitchen.

Clara opened the patio door and stepped out to the deck. The cracks in the floorboards were dark. There were no lights on in the bedrooms below. Looking up, she searched the beach line ahead of her.

"Avery must be in bed."

It had been a long time since Clara had walked the beach at night with Avery. She never liked the hours Avery chose even if it meant looking up at a sky full of stars. She liked sunset walks and even early morning walks on the beach with John. Witching hours with or without John were not good.

The breeze still blew, but it didn't refresh her as she hoped. It clung to her skin then sank into her lungs, making her breathe deeply. She moved back indoors. As she closed the door, she wondered why they had never put curtains on the windows, and then she wondered why she thought window curtains were important now. There was no one on the gulf waters to look inside the house, yet tonight she felt that she ought to draw curtains close over the windows. She took one last deep breath of the night air before sliding the glass door shut.

"What is wrong with me tonight?" she said, as a chill ran up her spine.

Someone knocked on the front door. The door bell ringing at one in the morning, while unusual, raised no alarms. Someone gently knocking on the door at one in the morning made the hairs on her spine tingle. Clara moved with caution toward the front door, glad for the light switch at the top of the stairs leading to the door. Through the peephole, a head of golden curls jostled in the sea breeze. She opened the door.

"Tommy? What are you doing here at this time of night?"

"Ms. Clara?" he said with surprise. "I knew you lived somewhere out here, but I didn't think I'd end up at your house."

"Well, come in. You're letting the night in." Clara hadn't meant to sound so relieved. "What are you doing out here?"

"Afraid my car conked out on me and, naturally, my phone's dead. There're a bunch of us meeting up at Surfside. Probably one of them will see me on the side of the road, but with my luck going the way it is, figured I'd better find a way to call someone. Hope I didn't give anybody a fright. This was the closest house I could see with any lights on. Hoped I'd find somebody up so I could use the phone. That's why I knocked. I figured if anybody was asleep I wouldn't wake them up with the bell."

"Now what kind of friends are you going to meet at Surfside this time of night?" Clara laughed at her fuddy-duddiness. How many times had her mother said those words?

"Yes, ma'am, well..."

"I'm just giving you a hard time. Can't help myself. The phone's over here."

Clara led him to the phone on the kitchen bar.

Tommy nodded to the television. "You're a fan of old movies?"

Bela Lugosi, black cape flowing, carried the damsel down a long curved staircase.

"I've been asleep. No idea what's on. Too much paperwork to do."

Clara started picking up the files from the floor.

"Don't you have a secretary to do that for you?"

Clara didn't answer but mumbled conspiracy under her breath.

Tommy finished his call. "Thanks for the phone, Ms. Clara. My friend is coming to help me out. I'll be getting out of your way."

"Why don't you stay in here? It's not a good idea to be hanging out on the road this time of night."

"I don't want my friend to miss me. He says he's close. Besides, it looks like you're ready to go to bed."

"Oh, don't bother about me. With the nap I just had, I'll be lucky to get back to sleep before the sun comes up."

"I really better get going, Ms. Clara."

There was no good reason for Tommy to stay in the house. "All right, but take this." She opened the little closet next to the kitchen and pulled out the big flashlight they kept for the storm season. "I don't want you walking into anything."

Tommy accepted the flashlight with a smile and turned to leave. "Thanks, and I'm glad I didn't wake anybody up." He stopped before opening the door. "I forgot. You live here with Ms. Avery, don't you? Can I say hi to her, too?"

Clara tried not to grin as she realized Tommy had a crush on Avery. Most men did. "This time of night, there's no waking her. She sleeps like the dead, but I'll tell her you stopped by."

"Well, I'd better get out to my car."

Clara watched Tommy move away from the house until he disappeared into the darkness. As soon as he was out of range she closed and locked the door. The tingling had moved up her spine to the back of her head.

The need for company unsettled her. Clara made her way to Avery's room and knocked. No one answered. Opening the door, she peeked inside. After the revelation earlier that evening, she was not sure Avery would be alone. The window curtains tossed in the breeze. The bed curtains remained neatly folded on the bedposts. Clara loved the massive antique bed, but there was no one sleeping in it.

Clara closed Avery's door. In her own room, she pulled the window curtains closed and pulled the bedcovers to her chin. She picked up the phone to call John but couldn't press the call button. She set the phone down and tried to relax. The wind blew, and the surf splashed, but there was no comfort in the familiar sounds. She picked up the phone again and this time hit the call button. Voice mail. She needed contact, even if mechanical.

"Well I guess you are either asleep at your desk or really working. I'm thinking about you tonight."

She tried to sleep, but every time she closed her eyes she saw Bela Lugosi's eyes peering in from the window.

*****

"Lights out, kiddo."

Mandy reached down to pull the covers up around Beau.

"Just let me finish this chapter, pleeeeeesssssee," he exclaimed, with brown eyes widening into those irresistible puppy eyes he always invoked when he wanted his own way.

"You said that half an hour ago. It's time good little boys went to sleep." Mandy hated being the disciplinarian, but she knew that Lizzie always fell for those beautiful eyes of his. She took the tablet from him and turned it off as she sat down on the edge of his bed. "I'll set this in the charging station for you."

"You're only doing that, so I won't read under the covers," he said.

"I can't pull anything over on you, can I?"

She tickled him then bent over to give him a kiss.

"How long will you be gone this time?" he asked.

"A day or two. Can I count on you to look after Mommy Lizzie and Sammy?"

"Sammy is such a pain in the ass."

"Mouth, little man! Your sister is very little and needs a big brother to watch over her. And she doesn't need to hear bad words from you. Got that?"

"Yes, ma'am."

Beau suddenly looked much younger and smaller than his nine years. Mandy could never be angry with him for more than two minutes.

"Can I get a kiss and hug before I go?"

Beau jumped out from the covers and swallowed her in a hug before she finished her question. "Bye, Mommy! Be safe and don't have too much fun without me."

He plopped back under the covers and fell asleep in minutes.

Mandy turned out the light on the bedside table and checked that the curtains were closed. Since she had returned home from visiting Celia, she found herself continually checking that the windows were locked and curtains closed.

She tiptoed into Sammy's room. The four-year-old slept hard with Bear and Dolly wrapped tightly in her little arms. Mandy straightened the covers of her bed and kissed her daughter good night. A shadow moved behind the curtains. Her heart raced. She looked up quickly, but it was gone. Mandy lifted the little curtain out of the way to see out. The street light was bright. There were no shadows outside her daughter's window.

"You're making me nervous," Lizzie whispered as she watched Mandy looking out of their daughter's window.

Mandy closed the curtain and followed Lizzie to the kitchen. "Sorry, hon. Got creeped out over nothing earlier, and it hasn't left me. That's all."

She began stuffing belongings into her pockets.

"Bullshit. You've been edgy for two days, ever since Dietrich pegged you for that special detail. I'm not asking any questions, but maybe you should talk to him about another assignment."

"Already have. Where's my phone?"

Lizzie lifted the phone from the charger on the bar and handed it to Mandy. "And?"

"It's cool. As soon as this job's done, we shut down here. I don't have to stay with it in Galveston. Even Dietrich is taking a vacation."

"That old goat doesn't know how to take a vacation. How he begot children is still a mystery to me. His wife must have jumped him between meetings."

Lizzie always made Mandy laugh when she needed to. And for a few minutes, she allowed herself to forget moving shadows, but she couldn't forget seeing Haskin's body or Celia's eyes when she saw Dietrich and Mandy walking toward her front door.

Mandy gave Lizzie and extra-long kiss goodbye that night. "I'll be back in forty-eight hours tops."

"You better be."

Lizzie waved, closed, and locked the door. It would be a long forty-eight hours, but she needed to make the casserole for the Haskins family, and she wanted to bake a cake for the kids. Chocolate cake with cheese puff filling was the favorite when Mommy Mandy was away.

*****

Dr. Charles Cross sat on the edge of his chair waiting for Dr. Keats. Stacks of overfilled manila folders balanced on his lap. He held his right hand at his mouth biting his nails, then he quickly put his hand under the files to stop the biting, but that caused his left leg to bounce, and the files quickly fell to the floor. Keats found him on the floor gathering papers.

"Still dealing with paper files, Doctor? I told you to convert them all to e-copy. I need quick access to information. It's a waste of time waiting for others to get you what you need."

Keats easily slipped into his desk chair and turned on the tablet.

"Already done." Cross continued to gather files. "I thought you might want the hard copies for your records."

"Leave them with Alice. She'll see they're filed. Are we ready for the transfer?"

"He's very nervous. He's worried that someone is going to hurt him." Cross regained the edge of his chair, but his leg still bounced. "I think it's all the guns. They are a bit nerve-racking if you're not used to them."

"Knock him out for the trip. I don't want any accidents." Keats stared at Cross for a moment. "Give yourself some valium while you're at it. It will stop your twitching."

"Yes, well ... is there anything else you need before we go?"

Cross stood up to leave, his eyes casting a longing glance at the door.

"You have your sample for me?"

"Oh, no," said Cross looking disappointed. "With all the excitement of the transfer, I forgot. There's not really much time now. We should wait till we get to the new lab."

"Now." Keats stood up and began to walk to the door of the lab. "I won't take any chances with your health, Charles. I rely on you too much."

Cross placed the files on the meeting table and started to the lab door, unsure whether he was glad that he was needed or upset about having blood drawn so close to the time to leave.

"I don't want the files in here. Take them with you."

Keats opened the door to the lab. The lights came on as he entered the room.

Keats liked this private entrance to the lab. He could come and go as he pleased without having to go through more guards. He could also work whenever he wanted. The lab was empty now, quiet, the best time to get real work done. Those going to Galveston had left in the afternoon. The others would be in tomorrow to clear up any remaining evidence from the specimen and send it to Keats. Automatically, he grabbed the lab coat from its peg next to the door and proceeded to pull out the blood draw kit.

"I'm ready," he said as he sat on a stool next to a workbench.

Cross set the files on the corner of another bench and sat on the stool opposite from Keats. He slowly unbuttoned the cuffs of his shirt and rolled up his sleeves.

Keats methodically prodded Cross's forearms with gloved hands. "They're not healing as well as they did at first. Any pain?"

Cross closed his eyes and squinted his face slightly. "Uncomfortable, a bit."

"Afraid we can't risk anymore damage to the veins. I'll have to draw from your leg. Perhaps it's time to consider getting someone else —."

"No!" Cross cut off Keats. "He wouldn't like it. He trusts me. Change now, and we'll have to start developing the trust all over again."

Cross began to wheeze. He pulled out his inhaler and puffed twice, embracing the medication and calming his breathing.

"I understand your concern for the boy, but I won't let you damage yourself. You're a brilliant virologist, and I need you if we're going to make this work."

Cross didn't listen. He bent over and began to take off his right shoe. "We should make the draw from the ankle."

Keats waited patiently while Cross rolled up his pant leg. Finally, Cross lifted his leg up and placed it on Keats's lap. Keats tightened the tourniquet above the ankle. He carefully found the vein and inserted the needle. Cross's eyes watered as the needle plunged in, but he made no sound as the vacuum tube quickly filled.

"Done. We still have several hours before we leave. Get some rest. I don't like your color. Are you taking the vitamins I prescribed?"

"Yes. And I will. I'll just check in on Jason once more, reassure him that everything is alright."

Cross gathered his files and limped out of the lab.

*****

"I've never been to Texas." Jason's speech slurred, and his eyelids drooped from the sedative. "Will there be cowboys, Charlie?"

"I don't know. We'll be on the island of Galveston. It's full of tourists. Maybe there will be some cowboys on vacation."

Cross rubbed Jason's hand. The coldness of the boy's hands still shocked him.

"I don't remember being anywhere other than California. Could I have been in Texas before, Charlie? You would tell if you found out anything about me, wouldn't you? It's lonely not knowing where you're from."

"Stop fighting the sedative. Close your eyes and go to sleep. I'll tell you everything."

Cross took out his inhaler and breathed in the medicine. He worried about Jason.

Keats reached down and checked the boy's carotid pulse. "Good. You can stop holding his hand now."

"The dose was almost double from the last time."

"Expected. You gave him the dose I told you to?"

"Yes. But ..." Cross wiped the sweat off his brow with his hand, then noticed Keats's disapproving face and grabbed his handkerchief. "What if we give him too much?"

"We won't. I check all the calculation myself."

Colonel Dietrich led Captain Hill and four soldiers into the cell. Cross began shaking as the soldiers lifted Jason to sitting and clasped steel bands around his wrist and bound them to his waist. Next, they bound his ankles with shackles.

"He's sedated. This really isn't necessary —"

"I'm ordered to deliver you and the package safely to Galveston," said Captain Hill.

"And doing an excellent job, Captain." Keats looked at Dietrich. "I'll be leaving then. Colonel Dietrich, it was good working with you. Cross, leave the captain to her work."

He and Dietrich shook hands. Cross followed Keats out of the cell stopping as he reached the hall to look back as two of the soldiers lifted Jason and half dragged, half carried him out of the cell.

Dietrich walked with Captain Hill to the loading bay where the truck waited. "Keep it out of the sun as much as you can."

"Yes, sir."

Captain Hill was good at her job, and she liked doing her job, but she hated this assignment. Colonel Espinoza had given it to her, and she appreciated his confidence in her abilities, but wished he didn't think so highly of her. Colonel Dietrich briefed her on the details, but she still couldn't wrap her head around it. None of this was possible. At least she was no longer seeing figures moving in the shadows.

"And, Captain," Dietrich lowered his voice and nodded for them to step away from the others. He pulled out a cigarette and held it tightly in his hand.

"Sir," Captain Hill wished she hadn't promised Lizzie and the kids that she wouldn't smoke anymore.

"You may be aware of rumors concerning Keats. They're all true, but I'm sure you can be diplomatic."

"Yes, sir. I was aware he was a prick the moment I met him."

Dietrich smiled. Captain. Hill was always honest. He tossed the cigarette on the ground. "Mind your mouth, Captain."

"Yes, sir."

Captain Hill made sure the back of the truck was secure. Keats and Cross sat in a nearby jeep. She signaled to her sergeant. The truck and jeep engines started. She hoped that Keats would be the only problem during the transfer.

"God bless, Captain, and see you home safe," yelled Dietrich over the engine noise.

Captain Hill turned and saluted her colonel. She suddenly disliked this assignment even more.

* * * * *

The young man in ratty blue jeans and sleeveless t-shirt on the fifth floor of the parking garage leaned against the lamppost incredibly bored and lit another cigarette. Despite the late hour, the top floor of the parking garage was almost full. The girl got out of the back seat of the car closest to him and combed her hair with her fingers.

"We should get back inside," she said. "Mama is waiting for us."

"Christ! Can't I get a few minutes to myself? Tell her I'll be in soon. Anyway, it stinks in there. And it's not like the old man is going to wake up anytime soon. Shit, he's been dying from that same damn tumor for ten years."

"Donny! I swear. Your mama wants you there. It's her brother that's dying. The least you can do is be with her. It's not like anyone's asking you to give a liver or something to the old guy."

"You don't give livers, stupid."

"You're meeting a girl out here, aren't you?"

"Will you just fucking go in, woman? The guy I talked to will be here soon. He says he's got some good shit. I'll score then be in. Now, will you go inside already?"

The girl grew quiet and her lips formed a large pout. "Will you save some for me, sweetie?"

"Don't I always? Now, get out of here."

The girl smiled and headed to the elevator. Avery watched the girl walk past without noticing the figure in the shadow. The elevator doors opened, and the girl went in. She smiled and waved at the boy as the doors closed.

Once again, his incredibly bored self leaned against the lamppost. Avery studied him. He and the girl had smoked a little weed in the car. His eyes drooped under heavy lids. His hair floated about his head uncontrolled. There was nothing remarkable about the young man. He tried to blow smoke rings but failed. He checked his watch and blew out more smoke. Finally, he started pacing. He checked his watch with each turnaround. He didn't notice Harry.

Avery watched as Harry moved without effort from shadow to shadow unseen by the young man until his pacing crossed within the shadow that was Harry. There was no sound of surprise. Avery listened to the silence of death. She breathed in the aroma of the young man — his sweat, his smoke, his blood. It filled her senses. And then, she could not breathe in. Darkness filled her vision. Her own life emptied from her body. An icy grip seized her arms. Her body shook.

Harry kissed her lips and squeezed her to him. "Breathe!"

She gasped. Warmth once again flowed through her body as air entered her lungs and exited her mouth. "I need you alive for one more day. You've controlled it this long. Just a little longer."

"A little longer. Yes. A little longer."

She rested against him, letting him wrap his arms around her and stroke her long hair. He was terrifying and beautiful to her. His very presence sent chills along the spines of anyone who passed near him, but for Avery this great fear comforted her. It filled her with courage and hope. With him, she was home.

"And when it's time, I'll take care of you. Don't be afraid."

"I'm not afraid."

Harry gave her a moment to collect herself. "Come," he said, taking her hand, "show me this colonel of yours. Convince me he should live."

They walked down the stairs to the fourth floor and stood close to the wall, watching as John walked between the hospital building and the parking garage. They saw him studying the garage. His gaze halted on the darkness of the fourth floor.

"He knows we're here, doesn't he?" she asked.

"A true warrior trusts his instincts. He survives by using the senses others try to hide. It's what makes him good at his job. But it's not us he senses."

Harry pointed to the smallest but fullest of the trees on the small mound.

Avery glimpsed golden curls hidden in the tree. "He's trouble."

"He has his uses. I'll make sure he leaves you alone."

"And Clara?"

Avery looked directly at Harry.

"As long as she knows her place."

A car drove to the front of the hospital and honked its horn. John turned his head to look. The golden curls in the tree, Harry, and Avery disappeared into the shadows.

*****

Everything was ready. At least everything was as ready as possible considering the uniqueness of the assignment. The truck would arrive within the hour. It should have arrived hours ago, but storms over the Rockies forced the flight to be diverted. John held the coffee mug under his nose and breathed in the rich, black aroma of the coffee. Typically, at this point in an operation John's mind wandered. He could only imagine what his soldiers thought about this assignment. Nothing to do now but wait. He set the mug on his desk and stood. *Time to walk the perimeter.* His back ached from sitting too long. *Would I have been this tired ten years ago?*

He walked out of Sealy Towers through the back doors that led to the courtyard between the little chapel and the cafeteria. The air hung thick, sticking to his skin and his clothes. He stood still, waiting. The light over the door made an annoying hum. It popped, flashed, and steadily regained its glow. Still, he stood. The air was too heavy to move. He listened to the sound of the traffic on Seawall Boulevard and Broadway. Tomorrow night weekenders and teenagers would fill the roads of Galveston. After a moment, he made out the white crests of small waves rolling onto the beach from the reflection of condominium lights and the sounds of the gulls calling in the dark above the noise of traffic.

John walked. He needed to concentrate. Too many depended on him to keep them safe. He needed to be sharp. Even in the courtyard of the Sealy Towers there were dangers in the depths of the night. Two nurses walked past him, gossiping on their way to the cafeteria. They were two more possible victims if he did not do his job. He focused on the activities around him and the sounds of their voices.

"He's such an ass!" said one.

"Tell me about it. He hasn't been here a week, and he's already laying it on that he knows what we need to be doing."

"Please! I hear he did nothing more than empty bedpans before he got his fancy degree. Like that qualifies him to tell me how to do my job."

John listened and smiled. As long as he did his job well, they would never know about the danger drawing near the hospital. He took out his phone to text Clara, the reason he worried tonight, and then he laughed at himself and put his phone away. *I'd chew out any of my soldiers if I saw them texting on duty.*

He turned the corner heading to the main tower entrance at the front of the hospital. Two men stood at the front of the doors talking quietly to themselves. They automatically pulled their shoulders back and stood up just a little taller as he passed. His men were trained well to be inconspicuous. He walked past the little hill covered with the oaks. A car turned into the front driveway leading to the entrance. John watched as the headlights sent beams gliding up the side of the parking garage. The fourth floor lights were out. The last thing he needed was someone getting mugged on campus. First, secure the package. Then he noticed a glimmer in the darkness of the fourth floor.

The lights of the car reflected off something. Pin lights? Reflectors? He strained his eyes. The flicker had come from a shadow within the shadows of the fourth-floor. The car honked its horn and screeched to a stop. John turned to face the entrance. The driver jumped out and ran to the passenger side. He helped his pregnant wife out of the car.

"It's our first!" he exclaimed to everyone standing near the entrance, a large grin on his face.

John turned back to look up to the fourth floor of the garage. The lights flickered then came on. *Just another floor in a public parking garage. Stop seeing problems where there are none.*

He turned his attention to the immediate area. The stand of trees brought him a moment's peace. He liked trees. They reminded him of when he was a boy climbing high in the old oak trees to hide. Sergeant or Mrs. Espinoza, his foster parents, always found him in the trees when it was time for chores. They would pretend to look for him, but he knew how long he could stay in the trees before play ended and it was time for chores. The Espinozas provided the comfort and discipline that made him the man he was today.

Tonight, he gazed up at the trees and imagined himself hiding and laughing where no one could bring him reports to write, contracts to sign, or duty rosters to review. Hiding in these trees meant no more contingency plans, no more planning for the worse. He smiled then noticed how the shadows among the branches created figures. The tree closest to him was the best for hiding in. It wasn't as large as the others, but it was bushier. Someone crouched on the upper limbs, waiting to pounce, or was it his imagination that formed the figure hiding in the tree? The hairs on his neck stiffened. His heartbeat quickened. He focused his eyes. From behind him, the distinctive sound of the army truck clamored its way from the street into the loading bay. John breathed in deeply. Shadows were only shadows. He quickened his gait to the loading bay but didn't hurry into the hospital: Always cool, always in control, but avoiding passing under the tree closest to him.

*****

The two sergeants stood in a small alcove near the loading dock door. The alcove was dark and filled with stacks of empty boxes. The men could be seen but not heard.

"You understand anything that Davis kid was talking about?" asked Emanuel Granton as he leaned his right arm against the wall.

"Hell no," replied Vincent Harris. "There was a time when shit like that interested me. These days, it just flies over my head."

"No shit. Still, he seems to know what he's doing."

"I'll give him that. You know when my littlest, Charlotte, was doing that robot thing at school last spring, Davis was one of the volunteers. He sounded just like the kids, going on and on about programming. He made it sound easy. Never saw Charlotte so excited about computer science."

"Maybe she'll grow up to build robots that'll take over our jobs."

Between the heaviness in the air, the expectation of the delivery, and the overall reluctance to believe what they were doing, they did not manage more than an attempted laugh.

"If you had told me about this six months ago, I would have called the medics for you," said Granton as he adjusted the cap on his head.

A movement to his left caught his eye. He turned his head slightly without looking directly at the offending soldier. He deepened his voice two octaves. "That's not a woman in your hands, soldier. Hold it like you know how to use it."

"Yes, Sergeant."

"Can't really blame 'em for being jumpy." Harris always spoke softly to his friend. "I mean, shit, I still can't get my head around it. You've seen the pictures of it? What the hell are we going to do when it gets here?"

"Keep a straight face, brother, and try not to shit ourselves."

Granton put his hand on the handle of the handgun on his hip.

"Amen. You know, I don't think even Espinoza knew what to expect when he first brought us in."

A radio squawked in Harris's hand and Lieutenant Davis's voice blared out. "Package has crossed the causeway. ETA ten minutes."

"Roger that." Harris turned to Granton. "Where's Espinoza?"

"Walking the perimeter."

"Not enough cameras for him to watch?"

"It's his way, always walks the perimeter before a package arrives. Stays cool. Keeps the soldiers in check. He loves his tech, but he doesn't forget his men — like others."

"Like Dietrich, you mean. If ever a man could get so turned around by tech. Davis sticks with Espinoza and he'll be okay."

"Remember when packing tech for an assignment meant packing weapons?"

"Remember the first geeks we had to work with? Drove me nuts! Always wandering around and not listening to us and then getting shot at."

The silence hung heavily between them. Talking about anything other than the soon-to-arrive package usually relaxed them. They had to work hard at it tonight.

"Still," began Granton, "geeks like Davis are now kind of scary. Sure, they're regular army and don't give us shit, but they are too damn smart. Kind of spooky if you think about it."

The radio in Harris's hand squawked again. "Package on property. Standby."

Granton kissed the crucifix hanging around his neck then tucked it under his shirt. He straightened up to his full height.

Harris closed his eyes and breathed in deeply. "No more shitting around. Let's show them how it's done."

"Let's get a move on, soldiers."

"Places! Let's go."

"Get off your asses! In places now!"

"You, secure the elevator. Move it!"

Every soldier followed the drill they had practiced so many times they didn't have to think about it. Every soldier breathed automatically. Every soldier waited expectantly but didn't want to see what would come out of the truck.

*****

In the loading bay, Sergeant Harris and his soldiers stood guard just inside the doors. Each held a shotgun, ready. Sergeant Granton opened the back of the truck. Many of the soldiers fidgeted and ran their fingers over the triggers of their guns. Sergeant Granton remained collected. When his gaze fell on one of his soldiers, he stopped fidgeting. John had worked with Granton many times over the years. Granton was always cool and in control. That's why John chose him for this assignment. The soldiers needed someone experienced and steady to help them in this assignment more than in any other. How often did a lifetime of illusion vaporize?

Captain Black disembarked from the truck first, tablet in hand and forms open, ready to document the official delivery of the package. If he was nervous, it was about paperwork being completed correctly. Regardless of Espinoza's opinion of Black, he appreciated his efficiency.

Captain Hill staggered out of the back of the truck, tired but alert and too tense. John insisted that Hill bring the package to Galveston, as she was one of the best security officers he had under his command.

Four men followed her, each as frazzled as Captain Hill. The package, surrounded by four soldiers, disembarked.

Despite studying the files, John had to work to hide the natural flinch he felt as it came out of the truck. Jason was just a kid — not more than nineteen years old. Even Jason was not certain how old he was. He had been on the streets since running away from a foster home as a kid. That was why John found it hard to think of this kid as a threat. They both had been foster kids raised on the streets. John was the lucky one. He got off the streets when Sergeant and Mrs. Espinoza took him in.

Red, frizzled hair hung scattered and tossed around a pale and freckled face. Dark circles framed his eyes. His shoulders drooped under a burden that John would never understand. The boyish frame barely supported him let alone the steel shackles that held his arms to his side and clanked at his feet. Two of the guards dragged him onto the landing. *How can this be a threat?*

Captain Hill released her prisoner to John. "It's all yours, Colonel. And I can't say I'm not glad to be rid of it."

The edge in her voice was clear. John did not remember it from other assignments.

"Any trouble along the way?"

"Most of the time quiet as a mouse. It got a bit nervous when we crossed the Causeway on to the island. We had more trouble with Cross constantly squirming around fretting over it."

When Dietrich briefed John on everyone concerned with the project, he spoke with as much disdain for Dr. Cross as Captain Hill had. Charles Cross's appearance did little to recommend him to John. Cross could burrow through the earth and never come out. He pulled his thin brown hair into a little ponytail. The remaining gray fuzz floated around his head. His face and hands were brown from too much sun that had aged him twenty years. According to his file, he was thirty-nine years old. He looked sixty and was about as tall as Captain Hill, who just made it into the army, but his squirming body made him appear shorter.

Cross darted after the soldiers taking Jason to the twelfth floor.

John needed to follow. Keats leaped out of the truck and moved to the elevators. John didn't want him telling his soldiers what to do.

"You and your men get some rest, Captain. I'll need a report in the morning."

"If you don't mind, Colonel, we'd like to head back as soon as possible. If there's a free office, I can get your report done in a couple of hours and then leave tonight."

John studied Captain Hill and her men. Despite the fatigue, they were eager to start the long haul back to California. He wasn't sure what took him more by surprise, soldiers not taking advantage of a layover in a vacation town or her nervousness. He wanted to be angry at the captain's lack of protocol. Then he remembered the shadows in the trees and the run on the beach.

"See Captain Black. He'll find you an office and arrange your return transport." John turned to leave.

"Thank you, sir." Captain Hill didn't hide the relief in her voice, but the watchfulness never left her eyes. "And sir..." she began.

John turned back.

She concluded, "Good luck to you."

"Thank you, Captain."

The "good luck" sounded more like a warning than an affirmation.

*****

John stepped off the freight elevator onto the twelfth floor. One of the first things he did upon arriving in Galveston was remove access to the eleventh and twelfth floors from the public elevators. Only those with keys could use these elevators. John fingered the keys in his pockets. *Too many people have elevator keys.* Security on the twelfth floor kept the average stray away from the project. The elevators opened into what was once a nurses' station. Lieutenant Davis established the control center for electronic surveillance and security of both floors in this area. He sat behind two rows of computer monitors and numbers keyboards. Clipboards for sign-in sheets and regulations appeared loosely set on the counter, but John knew Davis's eagle eyes would let no one pass without the proper identification or sign-in.

To the left was the north wing containing John's office and the offices for his administrators and some of the researchers. To the right, a wall separated the south wing, containing the labs and a secure cell for the project. Specialists Lewis and Carroll stood guard. The sight of these two soldiers holding weapons and watching everyone entering the floor provided John with peace of mind. He had picked these two specifically for this duty. He knew them and knew they took pride in their jobs. It showed.

"Davis," said John while walking behind the monitors.

"Sir," said Davis, anticipating his colonel's intentions. "Loading dock secure and package deposited."

"Anyone showing up who shouldn't be?"

John scanned the monitors as images from the loading dock and both floors flicked in black and white, color, and green in front of him. John insisted on the best technology to secure the area but still depended on humans for reassurance.

"Carroll, Lewis?"

"All clear, sir," snapped Specialist Lewis.

"All good, sir," said Specialist Carroll.

"Keep it that way."

John moved to the lab wing.

Specialist Carroll opened the door for him. John had laughed off the jokes Clara made about how entering a door guarded by Lewis and Carroll would be like entering Wonderland. Tonight the image of entering Wonderland shook through him. If Jason could be here, why not the Red Queen?

The tension in the air belied the outward appearance of calm. The guards' eyes darted from corner to corner to him and back to the dark corners of the hall. They were not standing at attention because he was in the hall. They were ready to move. Two guards stood at the end of the hall near the stairwell. John took no chances. He had sealed the door when he took over but kept guards on it at all times.

John recognized Corporal Checkers's shocking red hair even in the dim light of the hall. He couldn't see who stood watch with the corporal. Half-way down the hall, Specialists Vargas and Candida stood outside the secure cell. The door was open. Inside the room, Sergeant Granton supervised two soldiers, whose names John could not remember, release Jason's shackles and the steel band from his waist and wrists. *He's just a damn kid, but I know he's not. No wonder everyone is so tense. Clara was wrong, it's not Wonderland at all.*

*****

"You alone?" Colonel Dietrich still wore his Colonel's face.

"Stand by," said John as he nodded to Lieutenant Davis to leave the room.

It was Thursday. Sergeant Haskins was dead. Transfer of the package to Galveston Island shifted into high gear. The meeting was over. Everyone knew the parts they would play.

Davis checked an item off his to-do list on his iPad and made sure the door closed securely as he left the room. John switched the video of his old friend from the large monitor on the wall to his desk monitor and lowered the volume. He put his feet up on the desk.

"Hard to keep a straight face on with this one, Will."

"The whole damn thing freaks me out. Hell! Who wouldn't be freaking out when they found out about this thing? And I'd be lying if I didn't say I wasn't glad you were taking this over, John. But I sure as hell wish neither of us had anything to do with it."

Dietrich loosened his tie and poured himself a glass of whiskey.

"I know it's freaky, but we have to keep our heads clear. Keats says it's some sort of disorder. He'll get it under control, and we'll all laugh at ourselves for believing in ghost stories."

"Keats! Pompous ass. Find out what you can from that Cross fellow. He has his own ideas. If he wasn't such a nervous little toad, I'd find out what. I think he's a hell of a lot smarter than Keats, but he won't open his mouth. And until I know what killed Haskins, I'm leaving nothing, not even ghosts, out of the contingency plans." Dietrich refilled his whiskey glass. "You haven't seen it, been in the same room with it. You'll understand then. And don't give me that look, John. A couple of days with that thing under your watch, and you'll hit the bottle I know you keep in your desk."

"I'm not going to give you any shit, but Mary sure will when she smells that on your breath."

"Mary and the girls are going to visit her folks in Hawaii. I'm putting them on a plane in the morning. I'll head out there myself as soon as I can wrap up here. Sunshine and tropical breezes to cure the fear of shadows."

John put his feet on the ground, sitting up, and reached for his coffee mug. Will and Mary were never apart except when assignments forced them to be.

"You all right, Will?"

John could still wrap his head around what he needed to do. Years of dedication and training forged his mind into logical contingencies and balanced thoughts. Seeing and hearing his West Point friend and committed colleague suffer doubts and illogical conclusions frightened him.

"I will be, just as soon as this thing is away from here."

*****

As John walked into the observation room adjacent to the cell, he understood his old friend's wavering convictions.

Keats stood at the observation window smiling, his full attention devoted to watching the soldiers release the package's bonds. John wasn't sure that Keats was aware that he was stoking the cat in a gray, metal box. Neither spoke. The cat reached out its head, watching John with its brilliant, clear, green eyes. It ears were black. Otherwise, the cat was white. It reminded him of Avery, her clear green eyes, black hair, and pale white skin. Even the way it moved its head reminded him of her. Each movement purposeful, casual, and knowing. He liked cats. Clara was a veterinarian. *Why are there no pets in her house?* He took in a deep breath. He needed to keep his mind on his mission.

"Extraordinary, isn't it, Colonel?" started Keats. When John didn't reply, he continued. "Your Captain Hill was scrupulous but not very talkative. I found myself looking forward to more of our stimulating conversations."

"I understand the transfer went well."

The soldiers were leaving the cell. It was lit by a small light over the observation window. Jason sat despondent in a chair in the center of the room. He hung his head in his hands, but John watched as Jason scanned the room with his eyes. John noticed a slight arch of readiness in Jason's back, despite his appearance of weariness.

"This is your first time, isn't it, Colonel?" Keats smiled at John. "You're in for a treat. It's not every day that myths come alive." He switched on the microphone. "Hello, Jason."

Despite Will's warnings and the information others gave him, this was his first time to see the thing in person.

Jason looked toward the mirror. The lights reflected in his eyes making them glow red.

"Still amazes me," said Keats, turning off the microphone. "The physical changes have been slight but distinctive. They weren't there when I first saw him. Just your ordinary street urchin. Cross found the anomaly in the boy's blood. That's why he brought him to me. His eyes were always unusual, but now the way they reflect the light is unsettling. Wouldn't you say? Cross had a hell of a time finding him after I figured out what the anomaly meant. By then, the physical abnormalities you see had already begun forming."

"I'm sick," said Jason.

John looked hard at him. The observation mirror was one of the best made, but John suspected Jason looked right through it.

"It's all right, Jason," said Keats in the microphone. "Would you like something to eat?"

"Yes."

Jason's voice sounded weak and too young to be in the cell. John found it difficult to accept this kid was a monster. Keats pulled a bag of blood from a cooler behind him, put it in the transfer box between the two rooms, and slid the box into the cell.

"Here you are, Jason. This will make you feel better."

Jason's movements contradicted the tired look. He moved to the box, grabbed the bag, and turned his back to the mirror in one fluid motion. When he turned around John recognized not a tired, sick boy but a greedy young man out to get what he wanted.

"I need more." His voice was strong, no trace of weariness now. As if noticing the change within himself, Jason adjusted his tone. "Please. I'm sick," said the voice of a boy.

Keats turned toward John. "It doesn't seem to satisfy the hunger. The blood keeps him alive, perhaps, but it's the hunt he needs. Of course, we can't have him running the halls looking for his dinner, can we?"

John opened his mouth to comment when he noticed Keats placing the cat in the transfer box.

"Here you are, Jason. Since you were so good on your trip."

John held on to twenty-three years of training. Determination alone allowed him not to show any emotion or run out of the room retching. Jason opened the lid of the box, and the cat hissed and shrank into a corner of the box, but Jason moved fast and grabbed the cat before it could pull out its claws. Jason treasured his catch, bending over and sinking his teeth into its neck in one graceful movement. John kept his face expressionless as Jason lifted his head. His eyes glowed as he peered into the mirror at Keats. White fur and blood smeared his lips and chin, his mouth hidden in gruesome material, but John could still make out white, sharp teeth.

"More," came a different voice, distinctly animalistic.

"Watch," said Keats to John. "That's enough for now, Jason."

"More!" insisted the thing in the cell.

Jason advanced toward the mirror and hit it with his fist.

Keats pressed a button on the control panel. Hidden lights in the ceiling flashed into brightness.

"Stop!" shouted Jason, holding his arm up over his eyes and trying to find a dark corner.

The cat dangling in his other hand, lifeless. Keats pressed the button, and the light went out. Jason huddled in the far corner of the room shivering.

"We must learn to control our temper, Jason. You want me to help you, don't you?"

"Yes," came a quiet, frightened voice. "I'm sorry."

Jason petted the dead cat's head the same way Keats and been petting it a few minutes before. John wondered if Keats noticed.

Keats turned back to John. "Sunlight is bothersome to him. He can tolerate some, if he's well fed. I haven't had time to experiment thoroughly yet. For now, we just assume the myths contain some truths. Ever wonder about the old myths and legends, Colonel?"

John stared at Jason. Charles Cross entered the observation room carrying a clipboard with stacks of long lists. "Is everything going well?" he asked. He looked in the cell. Cross's expression mixed concern with pity. "Oh, yes, I see."

"He's calmed down," said Keats. "A little excitable after the trip. But we have an understanding, now."

"I see," said Cross, again. "Are these all the records of the samplings?" John noticed that Cross's eyes remained on Jason as he spoke. "You don't seem to have a large enough sampling."

"You can talk with Ms. Touluc about that." Keats made sure he stressed the *Ms.* "I'm sure *you'll* get along with her. What do you say, Colonel?"

If Keats was expecting a sly remark, John would not give it to him. "Ms. Touluc has been very helpful to us. If you'll see her in the morning, I'm sure she'll get the samples of blood you want. We included her in the project because of her past work with the blood bank. She's an effective recruiter and administrator."

Keats's satisfied smirk told John that Keats believed John's personal relationships were clouding his judgment. Before Keats could say anything, John changed the subject. "Has he mentioned the others again?"

"No," began Keats, "not since that one time. He refuses to talk about them now, but I'm sure he'll tell me all about them soon." Keats said.

Cross fumbled through the papers on the clipboard.

"At first, I assumed he was imagining them. But the more I thought about it... We are dealing with something from myth and fairy tales. I decided it was better and safer to accept the possibility of others. If we could find another like him—"

"One's enough for now."

The thought of another thing like this one excited John but not positively.

"A little disconcerting, isn't it? The thought of others like him in the real world."

"I don't want to take chances on *others* coming here. Keep me informed, Doctor."

"I suppose that's why I had to leave my comfortable lab in California to come here."

Keats rolled his eyes as he gestured to his surroundings.

"If the others were there, we don't want them finding us."

"Can you be sure they didn't follow us or that they aren't already here?"

"No and no," John said more matter-of-factly than he intended. "And since it's your project, I suggest you follow security protocol, just in case others are out there and don't like you experimenting on one of their own."

"I'll do my part, Colonel." Keats knew of the complaints against him and resented John for believing them. "As I'm sure you'll see everyone else does their part."

"You'll tell me when he talks about the 'others' again."

"Of course, Colonel."

Keats had to have the last word. John did his best to hide the signs of fatigue and disgust. His stomach continued to turn but not as much as it had been. Jason still crouched in the corner petting the dead cat.

Keats turned his attention back to Jason. "Put the cat in the box,

Jason. Dr. Cross is coming in for his daily sample. You should rest. I understand you have cable here. Wasn't that nice of someone?"

John walked out of the room to the cooler air of the hall. He paused long enough to take in a deep breath and force his stomach to settle. Sergeant Granton walked past him inspecting his soldiers. All it took was a glance from him to remind John that he had reports to read and reports to write and an image to maintain. For a moment it was acceptable to forget the thing in the cell, the dead cat that looked like Avery, and even Keats and his impossible conceitedness. John didn't become a colonel by doing everything himself. He had good men in place that would do their jobs well.

Back in his office, he logged into his computer and checked the security cameras. He flipped through every room on the eleventh and twelfth floors. The twelfth floor was quiet except for Lieutenant Davis talking to the two soldiers behind him. The eleventh floor was dark and filled with most of the civilian offices including Avery's. John always avoided looking into her domain. Before he came to Galveston, he hadn't considered looking into offices as invading someone's privacy.

"Get it together, Colonel," he told himself.

He switched the camera on in her office. Like the other offices, the lights were off except for the steady green lights of the monitor and computer. Reluctant but unable to resist, he clicked to view the cell.

*****

Amanda checked her watch, again. She texted each of them, again. The men she picked for this assignment were experienced and trustworthy. *Where the hell are they?* Reports were filed, the requisition for the SUV approved, and Captain Black had given her enough petty cash to ensure a hearty breakfast for all of them when they reached Ellington Field. The cash probably came from Espinoza. That was the type of thing he did.

If they fell asleep somewhere, I'll shoot each of them. They were all exhausted. What should have been a four-hour flight turned into an almost sixteen-hour ordeal. First, storms over the Rockies meant diverting the plane north. They had to go all the way to Great Falls to refuel. Next, came the thumping. The pilots didn't know what was causing it. The flight computers showed nothing out of the ordinary, but it was annoying as all hell. It sounded like someone banging on the belly of the plane trying to get in. They landed at McConnell. By then, it was midday. They were tired and hungry, but the package made it impossible to allow more than one person off the plane at a time, and she had to clear each mechanic and engineer who needed into the plane. The package remained quiet and behind the security wall. Still, those who came onboard knew there was something hidden behind a wall.

And the little shit just slept through the whole thing. She checked it frequently, and every time she did, she saw Beau's face entombed inside his favorite, fluffy pillow. His long eyelashes woven together in blissful, innocent sleep with eyeballs rolling around beneath their lids dreaming of baseball games, riding dragons, racing go-karts, and flying the X-wing fighter at Disney Land.

After all the delay of checking engines, wings, doors, and whatever the hell else needed to be checked out, it turned out to be a loose box in the hold. One of the pilots had picked up a Hollywood souvenir for his wife's birthday. Amanda wanted to chew him out, but he outranked her by three months.

By the time they reached Ellington Field, the weariness of the journey was taking its toll on most everyone. Captain Black, of course, didn't notice any delays. He read and read and read. And since he wasn't with security, he got off the plane at McConnell and didn't return until it was time to leave. To her surprise, Keats barely spoke to anyone. He asked her three times about possible arrival times, and that was it. He kept his fancy headphones on and read. He didn't even check on the package that was his project. He left that to Dr. Cross, who aggravated everyone by constantly wanting to open the door to check on the package. He would have stayed with it if she had allowed it, but Amanda knew better. The package was too dangerous. She didn't care that they appeared to be a little in love with each other. That only made the situation worse. *Another reason I hate men.*

Now, she had no idea where her own men were. They were supposed to stay on site but had asked to walk up to the Seawall. None of them had been to Galveston or seen the Gulf of Mexico. It seemed a reasonable request. They all wanted to go home, but after being cooped up on a plane for so long, she decided a little outing would do them good as long as they returned to the loading dock in two hours. That was three hours ago. She should report them to Espinoza, but that would be embarrassing and possibly damage her reputation.

I'll take a quick look myself. They're probably on their way back now. She drove the SUV, allowing the GPS to guide her to the Seawall. There were people hanging out at the pools at the various hotels, but otherwise the Seawall was quiet.

She pulled over next to a fishing pier. The store wasn't open yet, but a few fishermen stood along its edges with lines dangling loosely. She texted all her men again. No answer. She walked out on the pier.

"Ev'ning," said a black man wearing an ugly fishing hat.

"Evening," she replied.

"You're not AWOL are you Capt'n?" he chuckled at her.

She laughed back, "No, sir. Just taking some time while I can."

"I hear you, but don't be sir'ing me. Specialist, Infantry, First Cav, over twenty years. Sit yourself down." He stood up from the bucket he had been sitting on. "You look like you could use a break."

"Thanks, but what I could really use..."

"Say no more."

The man pulled out a pack of cigarettes.

"You are a godsend, soldier. Thank you."

He pulled out a lighter and helped her shield it from the wind as she lit the cigarette. "You know, I bet you're looking for some of yours. They were hollering it up a short time ago. Got themselves one too many, if you ask me."

"Little shits." She hadn't meant to say that out loud.

"They're behaving now. Cops pulled up a while ago, and they headed below." He pointed his head below the pier. "I bet they're still there."

Amanda handed him the package of cigarettes, but he refused.

"You look like you need them more than me. And I got plenty. Take them."

Amanda thanked him and headed toward the steps leading below the pier, determined to make her men sweat the long ride home.

Her men were not below the pier. She could make out empty beer bottles among the rocks reflecting what little light made it through the pier boards from the streetlights, but anyone could have put them there. She doubted the old soldier lied. *They've moved on. The shits!*

She sat on the rocks frustrated by her search. She would have to report to Espinoza that she had lost her men. Nothing but trouble from this trip. She lit another cigarette before her first one went out.

"Lost on purpose or accident?"

Amanda turned her head to see one of the most beautiful women she had ever seen sitting down on the steps just above her.

"Where—" she began.

"Everyone always says I move quietly, but you really are lost in your thoughts if you didn't hear me walking down the steps. You know, smoking is a filthy habit."

"That's what the kids say."

Amanda couldn't take her eyes off the woman. The lights from the street reflected a beautiful, long dark hair and silhouetted figure. While the woman's face was in shadow, Amanda could see high cheekbones, almond eyes, and luscious lips. She resisted, but her heart began to flutter.

The woman reached down and placed long, pale fingers on her right shoulder. Amanda felt a coolness run down her arm.

"I'm sorry," the woman said.

On her left shoulder, an icy claw gripped her. She felt the coldness surge through her body. Amanda continued to stare at the beautiful woman. She would not turn to see the face on her left, and then all she saw was darkness.

*****

By now, it was automatic. His people knew what he wanted in their reports. They did them right, and he only had to scan, click approve, and move on. He wasn't sure when the voice on the radio stopped and the music started again. It was the ringing phone that finally brought him back to consciousness.

"Espinoza," he answered.

"John?" It was Will Dietrich's voice, but not the voice of his old friend. It was tired and strained.

"Yes. What's wrong?"

"This whole thing is eating me up. I thought it couldn't get worse, but it just did."

"Tell me."

"I 've got have half a dozen dead. Maybe a few more. We're still cleaning things up."

John said nothing. He watched Jason sitting in his cell.

"Explosion and fire. Took down the whole complex. My folks say it appears to have started in the lab area, where the project was kept."

"When?" John needed facts. Will needed cues to stay focused.

"Around twenty-three hundred. It can't have been coincidence, can it?" Will didn't need him to answer. "One of the dead is a tech that worked closely with Keats and Cross. Pretty sure the others are our folks."

"Damn," was all John could say.

"I gotta go. It's a goddamn mess, John. Shit, I'm a mess. Can't even look at a shadow without jumping anymore. Take care of yourself. I'll keep you updated. For now, you know as much as I do."

"I'll ramp-up here."

"Better do more than ramp-up, John. Though how you'll prepare for... I don't know."

John hung up the phone and stared at the screen. *No doubt now. The others exist. Did they burn the lab? Why? If they were that close, then they knew the package had left. Or did they?* "Shit! Shit! Shit! You screwed up, Will."

He hadn't meant to say it out loud.

A shadow passed under his door along with the distinctive clicking of a woman in heels. He switched to the camera in the hall. No one. He checked the cameras in the other offices on twelve. Still nothing. He called to Lieutenant Davis.

"Yes, sir."

"How long since you last walked the hall?"

"Half an hour, sir."

"Do it again."

"Yes, sir. Dr. Cross wants in the cell."

"Let him in."

"Yes, sir. And Dr. Keats is on his way to see you."

The knock on the door was Keats, and he didn't wait for an answer. He walked in. "I need just another moment, Colonel. I assume you have a camera in the cell you can access from in here."

"Of course."

John turned on the cell camera as Keats walked around the desk to view the monitor.

"Jason is my project. You've been informed of my control over it?"

Cross entered the cell carrying a syringe on a tray. The guards stood inside the cell and closed the door behind them. Their eyes never left Jason.

"A good deal of control, yes." John didn't like the direction of the conversation.

"You're going to see something disturbing. Colonel Dietrich didn't like it any more than I did, but it is necessary. He was told that this is my call."

"Here we are, Jason," said Cross. "This won't hurt. We've done this lots of times. I can do this, and you never even feel the needle in your arm."

John thought Cross talked too fast.

"It became obvious early on that Jason wouldn't survive on cats and dogs. The human blood we give him helps, but it's not as fresh as he needs."

"Charlie," said Jason, "why won't it stop?"

"Dr. Keats is trying," said Cross.

"The first time Cross did it without my permission," continued Keats. "He monitored himself and Jason after each feeding."

"Give it time. If anyone can help you, Dr. Keats can."

Cross chatted without slowing about how Keats would cure Jason. John knew what was coming. He fixed his eyes on the monitor. He wouldn't let Keats see him flinch.

Cross spoke softly and maneuvered himself between Jason and the guards as he took Jason's arm and fixed the tourniquet. At the same time, he pulled up his sleeve.

"This will help."

Jason slowly put Cross's extended arm in his hand. "It's got to hurt."

"It's okay. We don't have a choice."

Jason didn't wait to protest anymore. He bit into Cross's arm.

"When did it start?" asked John.

"It's how Cross got Jason to come to us. We need him alive and thriving."

"You say you didn't discuss this with Dr. Cross before he started."

"This was all him. Set up a rather ingenious system to monitor himself after each feed. Obviously, I took over monitoring Cross. It has proven that the anomaly isn't transferred this way. Jason thinks it's their little secret. I'm keeping it that way for now."

Satisfied, Keats walked to the door.

"You will tell me if Cross develops any symptoms."

"I told you, Colonel, I monitor him myself. I will know if the anomaly transfers to Cross. I would have expected it to have done so by now. Lucky for Cross, it doesn't seem to transfer that way."

John was glad to see Keats leaving. "One more thing, Doctor."

"Yes?

Keats, agitated that John had shown no reaction to Jason feeding on Cross, turned back grudgingly.

"Your lab in LA burned down this evening. There are fatalities. No facts yet. Our people just started examining the wreckage."

"Then it's a good thing we moved when we did, Colonel. I copied my research files myself before leaving. The research won't be affected."

"Colonel Dietrich is sure it was arson."

"You think the others that Jason mentioned are behind it?"

"It's a possibility. It will take awhile before we know anything for certain."

Keats was quiet for a moment. "You mentioned fatalities. Any of my people?"

"One of your techs was in the lab."

"That would be Frank. He's a good man. Very dedicated. I'll miss him."

Keats turned to leave.

"One more thing, Doctor."

Annoyed, Keats turned back to John. "Yes?"

"Don't 'volunteer' anyone else to help feed the project."

Keats didn't reply.

Even if Keats did "volunteer" someone else, there was nothing John could do to stop it. The whole operation was too far-fetched for logic.

Lieutenant Davis rang John. "Hall's clear, sir. One of the men heard voices in the stairwell. Turned out to be a patient making a call. Sergeant Harris called in to say he found nothing wrong with the lights in the parking garage."

"Very good. I want a staff meeting in my office in fifteen minutes."

He pulled his phone from out of his pocket. It vibrated with a message. Clara had just called. He listened to the message twice, wishing he could call her back. It was three in the morning. The witching hours was what Clara called this time of morning. He wanted to rest for just a few minutes. He switched on the radio and turned off the monitor. He rested his eyes and listened to the music. Just a few minutes of rest to the soothing voice of the late-night DJ.

4

Along the beach at the end of the Seawall, in the shadows of the fishing pier, near the rocks next to the road, in an inlet of the rising tide, a seagull sits. The seagull's feathers fluff and blow in the calm sea breeze. A light comes on at the fishing pier. A woman turns on the radio and opens the shutters, casting light across the pier and through the cracks in the boards to the water below. A second seagull lands near the first and squawks. The sitting gull stands and squawks and flies away. The second seagull walks to the inlet and pecks at a soldier's cap floating in the pool.

Where were you when Hell came into town?
Were you standing on the street,
waving in the fanfare?
Did you take a peek?
Did you dare?
When reality and myth collide dreams disappear in shadows,
and the darkness of night becomes your only lead.
I'm Mary Midnight. You're at KMND Galveston.
I have the answers.
Victory lay your laurel down.
Hell never left this town.
Now there's a quandary for your dreams.

Clara woke with the sun blaring in her eyes. She fumbled for her phone. Eight o'clock.

"Shit!"

She wasn't sure when she had fallen asleep, but she felt as tired this morning as she had when she went to bed. Still, once awake, she was up. In fifteen minutes, she showered, put on jeans, an oversized button-down shirt, and tennis shoes.

"Grab the charger. Grab the charger," she repeated as she rushed to finish dressing.

Before she grabbed it, the phone rang.

"On my way," she answered.

There was no need to look at the incoming number.

"What do you want for breakfast?" Miguel laughed as he asked the question he always did and waited for the answer he always got.

"The usual. Make sure the coffee is strong. Be there in ten."

When she left her room, she noticed the stillness in the house and wondered where Avery was. She quietly opened the bedroom door. Avery was asleep in the bed. They had both slept late.

"Wake up," she said, striding into the room.

Avery stirred and muttered from beneath the covers. Clara pushed open the curtains. The sun streamed in.

"Hey!" Avery tightened her cocoon of covers.

"We're late," said Clara.

"I'm sick," said Avery, pulling up the sheets to hide her head.

"Of course you are. You stayed out all night. Do you want me to call the office for you?"

"I wasn't out all night. And no, I'll call later," Avery mumbled from somewhere under the covers or pillows.

Clara reached to pull the sheets back but streams of dark hair hid Avery's face. "Well, you weren't here when I went to bed."

"Yes, I was. You just didn't see me."

Avery moaned and went back to sleep. Clara looked at her for a moment, closed the curtains and tiptoed out of the room. She didn't have time to argue with someone who was asleep.

*****

John expected Cross to knock on his door, again, to ask after Avery. Sampling couldn't begin until she arrived and approved his taking the blood from the blood bank. Avery's absence didn't bother John. She kept her own schedule but got the job done. He left messages for her and Clara to call him in case Avery decided to take the day off. That was as much help as he could offer Cross today. He stretched his neck to keep it from drooping. The sound of his desk phone ringing startled him.

"What's up, sweetheart? I hear you've been looking for me."

As usual, Clara was cheerful and rushed.

"Yes, but only because I was looking for your friend. She's not here."

"Bummer. I thought you were calling to tell me we were going to Hawaii for the weekend."

John flinched when he thought of his old friend running to the Big Island. "That's next weekend." He hoped he sounded awake and casual.

"I can wait a week. Hang on." Clara spoke to one of her assistants, "Put him in the cage." She came back to the phone. "She should be getting there soon. I went home for lunch, and she was up and moving. She was mumbling about working late tonight. Though why she should want to go in on a Friday afternoon when the day is half gone. Hang on... IN THE CAGE! Sorry, anything else?"

A loud feline screech and a crash on the other end of the phone broke their conversation. "I told you she was in heat. Lock that ol' boy up before he trashes the place trying to get to her!"

John laughed.

"Sweetheart, I gotta' go."

Clara didn't wait for an answer before hanging up the phone.

John laughed for another minute, picturing Clara running after a cat. Then he pictured her running after a white cat with black ears. That made him think of Jason. John clicked over to the view of Jason's cell again. He couldn't stop himself from staring into that cell. Jason lay sleeping on the bed. Asleep, he looked even younger than he did when he was awake, even tossing and turning as he was now.

"How did that become a monster?" he wondered.

He switched on the camera to Avery's office. Darkness. The door opened, and he heard her talking to someone in the hall.

John used Avery's arrival as an excuse to leave his office. He needed sleep, but he needed company more. At the moment, he preferred the company of someone who made him forget white cats. He liked Avery because she made him laugh at himself. She disregarded security protocol as casually as he ignored her disregard of protocol, and she argued whenever he corrected her, but they were friends. They understood each other.

Avery was leaning back in her chair behind her desk. The blinds were closed and the lights were off. Only the glare from her computer monitor lit the room.

"Unless this is real important, it can wait till Monday."

"If I'm taking the trouble to come all the way down to your office, it's important." John hid the smile forming on his lips.

"Bite me."

"Did you get my e-mail regarding Cross?"

"I'm reading my e-mail now." Her eyes had not yet opened. "I cleared him to start the sampling before I left yesterday. What's his problem?"

"Don't shoot me. I'm just the messenger. What's the matter with you?"

"I have a headache and a busy afternoon. I don't have time to deal with petty things."

Charles Cross tapped on the door and opened it. "Excuse me, Colonel. Sergeant Granton told me Miss Touloc had arrived."

"It's Ms. Touloc, but call me Avery," she smiled at him.

The headache and busy afternoon washed off her face. John relaxed and stood back to watch her manipulate Cross with her charm as she had done to most of his officers.

"I need to speak with you about getting the samples from —"

"Everything is ready for you, Dr. Cross. Can I call you Charles? I'm so tired of doctors and colonels and sergeants. Aren't first names so much friendlier?"

"I'll leave you two to business. I'm in for a few hours sleep."

John could see Avery had Cross under control. Cross tried to keep his eyes down, but they kept creeping up to her shirt. Conveniently, Avery leaned toward him. She always left the top button of her blouses undone. Cross didn't stand a chance with her.

"Hey, take time to visit with Clara this evening." She didn't give him a chance to ask why. She turned back to Cross. "I'm sorry you didn't get my message. Were you waiting on me? I'd hate to think I held you up."

Avery wasn't sorry, and her attentions were making Cross nervous.

"Nothing that can't be remedied. I should get started." He turned to leave with John but stopped in the doorway. "There is one thing I noticed while checking on the records." He looked back to Avery but kept his head down. "You haven't given a blood sample."

"No? But I'm sure I did. I remember doing it right after your people got here."

"Everyone with the project is required to give samples for continuous screening."

John wondered whether Cross brought this up in front of him on purpose. He was more clever than John had thought.

"I'm not military."

"*Everyone*, Avery."

John let her slide on many issues but not this one. After what he'd seen last night, he was taking no chances that anyone else might become infected.

"No problem. I'll get Marissa. She can stick me."

"It has to be—"

"Marissa is one of your technicians. She's fully qualified, and she can do it, so I won't faint. Now you know one of my little secrets, I can't stand the sight of blood."

Avery stood, letting the slit on her skirt open as far as she wanted it to. Cross followed the slit up her thigh.

"Dr. Keats was specific when he said that I..." began Cross.

"Dr. Keats and I have an understanding," replied Avery. "Colonel Espinoza understands the arrangement. You two come with me right now, and we'll close the matter. How's that for security, Colonel?" She smiled at him when she said *colonel*.

"It works for me."

John was glad for the opportunity to make sure Avery gave her sample. She had the skill to talk Cross out of it.

Five technicians were busy around a center workbench in the lab Avery entered. A large woman at the far corner sat on a stool and hummed out loud. Otherwise, the room was quiet. John remembered that Keats had insisted on no radios in the labs.

"Marissa," Avery called as she walked up to the woman, "do you remember me saying I might ask a little favor of you?" She had taken off her jacket and rolled up her sleeve by now. She held out her arm. "Well, it's time."

"Girl, I don't know about you. Running away from little bitty needles, and at your age. Come sit over here."

Marissa pointed to a chair in the corner as she gathered a blood collection kit.

"I have a delicate disposition."

Avery flashed her best, charming grin. Marissa laughed. Avery made sure the slit on her skirt widened over her thigh as she sat. Cross noticed, too.

"Delicate disposition, my ass."

"You know you're the only one around here who can do this right."

John watched Marissa's face to avoid the needle and blood. He was too tired. Or maybe Avery reminded him too much of the white cat with the black ears.

"All done." Marissa put a piece of gauze inside Avery's elbow. "I'll just label this."

She grabbed a pen from her pocket.

"I can do that," Cross offered and reached toward Marissa's hands.

"Doctor, I've been doing this longer than you been wearing britches. A label on a tube of blood is simple enough to make. Let me do my job and not start handing around tubes of blood like they're candy. This is just as important as drawing the blood. Wouldn't you agree? Besides, what's that Dr. Keats always going on about? Accountability. He's been very specific about procedures for this sort of thing."

"Of course."

"Thank you so much," said Avery as Marissa handed the labeled tube to Cross. "You're such a dear. Now, unless you gentlemen need any more bodily fluids, I have a dozen e-mails to reply to, half a dozen phone calls to make, a spaghetti dinner to attend, and much to do to prepare for it. I might add, I could avoid this dinner if it were not for you two. Every member of the Knights of Columbus on the island will be at St. Patrick's tonight for the blood drive benefiting our beloved war veterans. It's such a big event that Father Chuck insists I be there to represent UTMB and say a few words, which you should be saying, since the purpose of the dinner is to collect the blood samples you want, Colonel. There is something about a man in a uniform. It's good PR. Did I ever tell you that I don't like spaghetti?"

"Everybody likes spaghetti," said Marissa, "at least when I make it."

"Well, if it's half as good as the scampi you brought to the mid-term party last year, I'd eat it. John, sleep. You look like shit. Charles, I enjoy talking with you, but I have so many things to do, and you have a sample to run." She moved like she spoke— smooth, direct, and vague. "Oh, and John, Clara will be at the dinner tonight. It really would boost donors if you showed up in your pretty uniform."

John accepted Avery's dismissal and went to the hotel. A few hours sleep would be perfect. He stopped once to leave a message with Clara telling her that he was at the apartment. He wanted to feel her presence, if only in a voice.

*****

Clara half dozed as she stretched out in the chair behind the desk. Gaston, lying on the floor beside her, stretched and yawned, too. She reached down to scratch behind his ears.

"It's been a long day, hasn't it, Gaston?" she said.

Laura, the high school receptionist, did her homework at the front desk. The other assistants and the groomer had gone for the day. They were waiting for the last patient. Clara thought she would nap, but the phone rang.

"It's Ms. Avery, Dr. Lucas," shouted Laura, although she was only a few feet away from the open door.

"What's up?" asked Clara, picking up the office phone.

"You left your charger at the house again, didn't you? I've left you several messages."

"Guilty."

Clara closed her eyes and saw the charger sitting on the dresser where she left it.

"Come out to St. Patrick's tonight. I could use the company."

"I'm still waiting on one more patient."

Friday night at a church social was not what she wanted to do.

"They're starting to set things up now. Maw Maw and Paw Paw got here a few minutes ago. Things won't get going for another hour at least. Oh, and Father Chuck mentioned that he hasn't seen you in a while."

"He would." Clara looked at the clock. "I don't know, I'm kinda tired."

"And I bet you're hungry. What could be better than free food.? Besides, if I have to be here on a Friday night, my best friend should at least share some of my misery."

"Speaking of best friends..."

"John's coming over later."

Clara wondered at that. John did not like public gatherings. Why would he show up at a spaghetti dinner for the Knights of Columbus?

"What's he doing there?"

"Secrets, secrets, secrets. If you don't want to come that's fine by me." Avery loved to overplay sincerity.

"Okay, I'll come."

"Good. Later."

Avery hung up without giving Clara time to ask why she had lied about being out all night.

*****

After an hour of tossing and turning, John gave up trying to sleep. A shower and a shave, and long drive along Seawall Boulevard on his Honda Shadow would clear his head, but tourists filled the road. Weekenders coasted up and down the boulevard admiring the brown gulf waters. Teenagers parked in clusters, admiring each other as they walked up and down the boulevard trying to look sexy, cool, or whatever teenagers were these days. So, he turned around and headed for the hospital.

Lieutenant Davis sat at his station on the twelfth floor when John arrived at the hospital.

"Did you get some downtime, Davis?"

"Yes, sir. Ready to go. Looks like it's been a busy day."

Of course, Davis was ready to go. John sighed as he remembered what it was like to be twenty-seven and involved in a top-secret assignment. Adrenaline and coffee kept him sharp, focused, and on top of his game.

Quietly, John asked, "Reports from LA?"

"A few, sir. They've been coming in all afternoon. Nothing definitive, yet."

"I'll be in my office."

Before reading reports, he logged in and turned on the camera in Jason's cell. Jason paced back and forth across the cell. Suddenly, he stopped, lay down on the bed, and fell asleep. "Wish I could sleep so well."

It didn't take long to read the reports from LA. It was too early for any conclusive evidence. Seven bodies were accounted for, all in or near the central lab. In Galveston, there was nothing unusual at the hospital or on the island.

John stared at the monitor, again. Did the explosion in LA have anything to do with Jason being moved? Did the kid sleeping in the maximum security cell in the middle of a heavily secured research facility know anything about it? John's head swam with questions. He needed coffee, and he needed answers. At least he could find coffee in the break room. He was already opening the door when he heard Keats and Cross talking. It was too late to turn around, so he took a deep breath and walked in.

"—but he's quiet now," Cross said to Keats.

"Got some rest, Colonel?" asked Keats. "I slept like a baby this afternoon — a hundred percent better. Can't keep the hours we did when we were young, can we?"

"No." John hated making pleasant conversation. "Everything quiet, here?"

He noticed Cross was pale and fatigued.

"Charles said that our boy gave him a bit of a worry this afternoon."

John became alarmed.

"Why didn't you call me?"

"Nothing to report," continued Keats. "Jason woke up nervous and irritable, probably having a bad dream."

"He woke up," said Cross, turning to John. "He was sleeping peacefully and then began to toss and turn. I haven't seen him do anything like that before. Jason usually sleeps peaceably during the day. But this afternoon, he suddenly got out of bed and began pacing. He told me it was nervous energy, but I didn't believe him."

John considered the information. Jason was a kid. He was a kid locked up under heavy security. He was a kid with a disease that made him a monster. Then again, he had spoken of others, and there was the explosion in LA.

"Does he dream?" he asked.

The myths stated that vampires were dead during the day.

"I don't see why not." began Keats, "His sleep patterns are, obviously, different from our own. You should ask your friend Dr. Lucas. Animals are her expertise. She might be able to give us an interesting insight."

He paused for a moment. "Unless you intend to move us again, I hope to find out these things."

"He's told me he dreams," said Cross directly to Keats. He liked knowing more than Keats. But then Cross told Keats everything, so John wasn't sure why Cross would feel smug. "He woke once and said he'd been dreaming of riding a motorcycle on the beach. He's never ridden a motorcycle and would like to."

"Interesting, but today — he's quiet now?" asked John.

"Yes, about five-thirty he went back to sleep."

"So all's well. No doubt our boy had an interesting life prior to being with us. He's living better now than he was on the streets," said Keats.

John filled his mug with coffee and began to leave, unable to imagine how anyone could consider Jason's present circumstances *better* than they had been. He may have been living on the streets, but there was no sign of drug use, and he wasn't a monster then.

"There *is* one thing, Colonel, before you leave."

Keats turned to Cross.

Cross spoke cautiously. "It concerns Ms. Touluc."

John hesitated. Leave it to Keats to find something trivial to anger him and then get someone else to do his dirty work.

"Yes?"

"Her medical file is empty. There are no blood samples on record to compare this one with."

"And this causes a problem, because?"

Cross spoke first. "The anomaly is difficult to trace. In Jason's first sample, I almost missed it. By comparing samples, it's easier to notice its development. This is why we ask for regular samples from everyone."

John took a deep breath before responding, relieved there was nothing more serious than a bad filing system. "Getting blood samples is your job. Don't like what you have, get another one."

"Colonel," Keats stood to make his point. "The file is *empty*. How did she get assigned without a physical?"

"I read reports on everyone involved before arriving in Galveston. One of your people must have checked her out."

"No one on my team remembers examining her," said Keats. "So, who signed the report?"

John found himself angry at Keats and Avery. "I don't recall. Only army doctors examined locals, but there are too many to remember all their names. Make some calls if it bothers you."

"I attempted to pull her medical records from the hospital," interrupted Cross, "but they can't be found."

"A state-run hospital can't find someone's records. Imagine that. Run another test, then talk to me. Follow up with your own people for misplaced or missing paperwork. Deal with it."

John left the room without giving them a chance to reply. Keats didn't like Avery. He almost had John believing in Avery's deliberate sabotage techniques. Avery, too, would have to give in a little. Rules were meant to be bent and molded to fit circumstances, but not broken without sufficient cause.

Captain Black waited for him outside his office. "Sir, I need a word with you."

"Come in, Captain."

He didn't mean to sound impatient, but he was angry, and the last thing he wanted to deal with was administration. John neither liked nor disliked Captain Black. He was a good administrative officer. When his twenty years were completed, he would no doubt become a very good bank administrator. He might even help John get a mortgage or maybe a fishing boat.

John sat down at his desk and logged back on his computer to clear his head. "Alright, I'm ready now."

But Captain Black had not come with paperwork. "It concerns Captain Hill and her men. They're missing."

John said nothing. He liked Captain Hill — thorough, efficient, good at her job. She wouldn't go missing. "Are you sure?"

"Yes, sir. They were in such a hurry to leave last night that I assumed they headed back to Ellington Field when she completed her report. I told her that the earliest transport left at 1800 today. I suggested that she and her men check into the hotel and to rest. Ordinarily, I would have expected them to take advantage of a day on the beach, but she said they wanted to leave as soon as possible.

"I received a call from the pilot of the transport at 1700 asking me where they were, as they had begun to load the plane. As I said, I'd assumed they drove back to Ellington Field last night. I've called around, but nothing. The pilot called again just before 1800 and said he had to go."

"You checked the hotels?"

"First thing. Nothing."

"Get on it. Take Harris and whoever else you need. Check with the locals but keep it quiet."

"Yes sir."

Captain Hill left. The knot in John's stomach grew tighter. He had disliked this project from the beginning. He understood now what made Will Dietrich send his family away. He pulled up the recordings of Jason's cell. At 1330, Jason sleeping peacefully. By 1400, tossing and turning in his bed. He jumps out of bed and paces. Cross spoke.

"What's wrong, Jason?"

"Nothing."

"Did you have another dream?"

"Sure. I had a bad dream. I just want to move around some, clear my head."

"Dr. Cross." John recognized the voice of Sergeant Granton over the speaker. "You asked me to keep you informed of when Ms. Touluc arrived. She's in her office now."

"Thank you. Sergeant I have to leave you for a little while, Jason. Try to relax. Get some sleep."

"Charlie," said Jason.

"Yes?"

"Never mind." Jason paced.

John wondered what made Jason nervous. Avery arrived in the building and Jason became nervous. She left and he became quiet. Coincidence. But Jason had relaxed about the same time Avery left the building. What happened to the file with the physical and the blood sample? He thought of the figures in the tree, the laughter on the beach, the woman's footsteps in an empty hall, and Captain Hill missing. All his certainties were changing.

He pressed the intercom. "Lieutenant."

"Yes, sir," came Lieutenant Davis's voice on the other end.

"Get a car. We're going out."

"Yes, sir," When hunting shadows, better to chase them all.

* * * * *

By seven forty-five Clara arrived at the Knights of Columbus Spaghetti Dinner and Blood Drive. The hall echoed with the sounds of people. She found her father in a corner with the other old men drinking orange juice and telling stories. No beer allowed until after nine o'clock since most of the men had given blood. As usual, Maw Maw orchestrated in the kitchen, stirring pots, checking the oven, picking up dishes, and telling the younger women how things should be done.

Clara maneuvered through the hall to the courtyard. It seemed to take hours. Everyone had to say hello and ask why she didn't come to these dinners more often. Too many patients, she said, too much to do. Once outside the hot night air was a relief from the frantic hall. She left through one of the smaller doors to avoid the crowd in front of the Bloodmobile and noticed the driver's side door of the large vehicle opening.

The crowds were on the other side of the vehicle. There were no lights on the driver's side, but Clara could make out Avery leaning out of the door looking for something. Clara started to shout to her but realized Avery probably wouldn't hear her, so she began to move toward the Bloodmobile. Then Clara froze. A figure in the shadows moved up from behind the door, Max. He stepped into the light of the vehicle and reached up to Avery, carefully carrying her to the ground. He had the look of someone up to no good, just as he had last night at the grocery store. Avery closed the door behind her, and they walked into the shadows.

Clara walked back into the hall. She didn't like Max and wished Avery didn't like him. All the years she and Avery had been friends, Avery had seldom involved herself with anyone. Until now Clara had thought little about it. She picked up a glass of iced tea and stood in a corner. There were too many wild thoughts going through her head to think straight. Someone grabbed her shoulder.

"John! You're here? I thought Avery was joking when she said you were coming."

"Avery told you I'd be here?"

"Why wouldn't she? Anyway, I'm glad you are."

"I need to find Avery."

Clara could see that John was on duty. Lieutenant Davis stood behind him.

"What's wrong?"

"Something's come up."

Clara knew John would say nothing else.

She hesitated for a moment. "She's out back."

"Let's look for her."

John led Clara outside. They moved away from the crowd. Lieutenant Davis stayed near the door.

"I'm sorry, Clara. But I have to find her. I don't know that she's done anything she shouldn't have, but I need answers."

"There you are." Avery walked up to them smiling. "Just wondering when you'd get here."

Clara wondered who Avery was talking to. *Why did she expect us to be here when, clearly, John had not planned on coming?*

"We need to talk," said John.

"Okay."

She always wore that same smile.

"What happened to your original blood sample?"

"This is a joke, right?"

"It's no joke, Avery."

"You witnessed Marissa taking a sample from me today. Lighten up a little? You're the one so hot on not talking shop outside the office. We are in a public place. And smile. As far as these people are concerned, you're here to meet and greet."

That damn smile. What is she up to? John looked to Clara for answers.

"I'm talking about the original blood sample and physical you took before the job began."

"You'll need to talk to your own people about that, John. All I did was show up, get a physical, give some blood, and leave. Your people handled all that paperwork."

Clara was deep in thought, but suddenly asked, "How did you get Marissa a job in a classified project?"

"Why shouldn't Marissa be on this project?" John asked Avery.

"You wanted me to get local technicians. I followed your rules. She's a good tech who made a mistake once. It's in the past," Avery added before Clara could respond.

"She fixed *drug tests*, Avery," said Clara.

"And served her time for making a mistake."

Avery appealed to Clara to drop the subject, but John knew what needed to be done.

"I want you to come to the lab and give another sample."

"This is ridiculous."

"She doesn't like needles, John," said Clara. "I'll go with you, Avery, and if you faint, I'll take care of you."

John hesitated. He didn't want Clara involved.

"What's that son-of-a-bitch Keats said to you that's got you so on edge?" Avery asked John.

She still smiled.

"Avery."

"Wait." Avery held up her hand. "Don't tell me. If Clara can come, I'll do it. Let's just get this settled."

Clara caught Avery scanning the shadows near the Bloodmobile. Clara turned to look in the same direction. If Max was still there, she didn't see him.

Lieutenant Davis drove the car. John sat up front with him. Avery and Clara sat in the back. No one spoke on their way to the hospital.

Radios blared from all the cars on the boulevard. The usual Friday night machinations drowned out any chance of conversation in the car. Victory rose before them as they made their way up Broadway. The Goddess refused to acknowledge them. As they drove past, Clara noticed that one of the spotlights shining on Victory was out. She thought she saw someone standing in the shadows.

You're losing it, girl.

5

A man with a purpose steps up to Victory. He removes his backpack and sits in the shadows of the statue where the lights are broken. He leans against her base and cools himself in her melancholy. Cars drive past. Some are noisy, some purr, some smoke. They fill the night with life's melody. A patrol car pulls in front of Victory. The man with a well-polished badge hands a ticket to a young man with a red car and a red face and five companions. He sees a backpack at Victory's base. He picks up the pack.

"No respect," he mutters, and puts it in the trunk. He eyes the Salvation Army on the corner with contempt.

I'm Mary Midnight. You're listening to KMND Galveston.
The players are taking the line;
the first move is made.
Will twilight disappear?
Does Knight take Queen,
Or does Queen take night?
That's the question we ask ourselves now.
Reality be damned.
The dream is the life.

"Do you have to do that?" asked Clara as she paced back and forth in front of Avery's desk.

"As long as I have to be in my office on a Friday night, I might as well take care of reports that have been piling up."

Clara couldn't decide who she was more annoyed with. Was it Avery for ignoring the seriousness of the situation, or John for putting her in this crazy situation?

Captain Black met them when they arrived at the Sealy Towers. He took John aside to talk to him. When John returned, he told them he had to handle a situation, and asked if they would mind waiting in Avery's office.

"In other words," began Avery, "I'm under house arrest."

Lieutenant Davis escorted them to Avery's office and left them. Sergeant Granton arrived before they had time to talk. He kindly offered his services as he was stationed at the end of the hall. Whatever John believed Avery had done must be serious. Avery's carefree attitude in the circumstances annoyed Clara. She was tired of pacing and being ignored.

"Can't you at least tell me what's going on?"

Avery turned to her, smiling. "None of this has anything to do with you. Unless you consider the fact that it's tearing John up inside and out to have you involved."

"That's not an answer."

"No, it's not."

Avery continued typing on her computer.

Not ready to abandon the discussion, Clara asked, "Why did you lie about being out last night?"

"Please! I was half asleep when I lied. Besides, I didn't leave you for long."

Avery continued typing.

"I really needed some company last night. Tommy doesn't count since he was hardly in the house ten minutes."

Avery stopped typing. "Tommy was in the house last night?"

"His car broke down. He came to the first house he found with lights on."

Avery stared out the window for a moment. Before she could speak John entered. He only looked at Clara.

"I'm sorry to ask you to wait."

"You have a hell of a lot of explaining to do." Clara's temper was reaching its edge.

"He's just doing his job, Clara. Now what do you need from me?"

"Cross says the blood sample he examined isn't yours."

Avery didn't act surprised.

"You witnessed Marissa take my blood. Well, sort of. You did go a little green."

"I saw your blood being drawn but not the writing on the tube."

"You're getting paranoid."

"There's also the matter of your physical. Keats can't find anyone on his team who remembers giving you one."

"It's not my problem if you can't keep up with your own people. Dr. Houseman did my physical. You met her in my office about two days before she went on maternity leave. Tell Keats to call her."

John's muscles tightened in his neck. "Why are there no medical records of you at the hospital?"

"Oh, please," exclaimed Clara. "Are you telling me you dragged us down here because of something that happened ten years ago?"

"Clara..." began John.

"Ten years ago, I had a bad case of the flu. Clara insisted I go to a doctor, although I didn't see any reason for it. Other than then, I've never been sick. Anyway, she arranged the appointment with Dr. Brackon. He decided that I didn't have the flu and ordered a bunch of tests."

"Why didn't you ask me?" interrupted Clara. "I was there. She couldn't stand up or keep anything down. Still, I had to drag her to the appointment. The next morning, this guy was all over the morning news. He jumped off the roof of this very building. You'll excuse the records department if a few files got lost in the confusion. Not that it mattered, she was fine in a few days. It turned out to just to be the flu."

"I still need another sample."

The agitation in John's voice came through loud and clear.

Before Avery answered, Sergeant Granton rushed in the door. "Sir, you're needed."

John left the room without a word, leaving the two women alone. A moment later Sergeant Granton came back in. "Excuse me. We've had a situation develop. The Colonel asks that you stay in the office and not try to leave. I'll be outside the door."

Despite her desire to remain calm and in control, Clara's chin fell and her breath quickened. The statement alarmed her, but the seriousness in the Sergeant spoke volumes. Avery, to Clara's frustration, turned back to her computer and resumed her work.

"What's going on?" she asked.

"I'm not at liberty to discuss that, ma'am."

"Not at liberty," her voice echoed, rising two octaves. "You come in here like a cloud of doom and you're not at liberty to discuss the matter?"

"He's just doing his job, Clara."

Clara rolled her eyes at Avery's apparent serenity. It wasn't the way she should be acting. Avery should be angry, but she wasn't. Granton left the room quickly.

"Don't start in on me," Clara snapped back to Avery, the volume of her voice continuing to rise. "First, I have to find out by accident that you're dating some biker. Then you flat out lie about going out last night. I saw you sneaking out of the Bloodmobile to go meet this guy. If you can't meet in the open, then there must be something wrong with him. I don't like him, and yes, I haven't actually met him. Don't interrupt. Then my boyfriend practically *arrests* you and drags you down here because you switched your blood sample. Now I've got the US Army standing guard over me. The least you can do is look at me when I'm talking to you!"

Avery had left her chair to face the window while Clara ranted.

If she was listening to Clara, she didn't comment. Eventually, she turned to Clara.

"You're my best friend, Clara; I always pay attention to what you say."

Avery sat back down at the computer.

"What are you doing there that is so god-awful important that you can't talk to me."

Clara walked around Avery's desk. On the computer monitor was a small room with a young man pacing and biting his nails.

"Are we supposed to see that?"

A coldness pressed the back of her neck. She turned to look behind her, but everything went dark.

*****

The knot that had been growing in John's stomach tightened since Granton entered the room. It had been bad enough listening to Captain Black explain that Captain Hill or her men had disappeared. Now Keats began to agitate him more than usual. Jason paced his cell again, mumbling about dying. "They're coming, tonight," he kept saying. "They're coming."

Who or what "they" were John could only guess. If "they" were responsible for Captain Hill's disappearance or the explosion in the LA lab, John had reason to worry. Now two of his own people were missing.

John stood outside the Sealy Hospital main entrance. A nurse cooed to a female patient who wouldn't stop crying.

"Monsters," the patient kept saying between sob. "I saw them, monsters with glowing eyes, and they took those men, right up into the trees."

Sergeant Harris and five others searched the trees with their flashlights. There was no sign of the two men posted out front.

"It's as though they were never *here*, sir," Sergeant Harris said.

"But they were here. Get back inside. Tell Captain Black I want Receiving secured."

"Yes, sir."

"It's okay," said the nurse to the patient. "There's nothing in the trees or those men would have found it. You need to get to sleep now. This is what happens when you're too tired, taking lots of medication, and then decide to smoke. The nicotine is playing tricks on you. Come back inside. I'll have the doctor prescribe something for you."

The patient slumped into his wheelchair. "I'm not smoking, ever again."

Inside the hospital, John examined every face as he walked through the lobby. Visiting hours were over, but there were still too many people who didn't belong. He thought of Clara and Avery on eleven. He wanted to get them out of the hospital, but he couldn't spare anyone to escort them, and what was Avery playing at? Keats may be an ass, but he was thorough. Avery had logical explanations for every suspect action Keats claimed, but her answers were *too* logical. It was as if those two were playing a game with each other, and John was caught in the middle. At least Granton was with Clara and Avery. He hoped that if the "others" came for Jason, they would leave floor eleven alone. *If I wanted to get to Jason on twelve, I would enter on eleven.*

The elevator stopped between the eighth and ninth floors. It went dark.

"Talk to me." he ordered on the radio.

Lieutenant Davis responded, "The whole hospital is out, sir. The generator should kick in any minute."

As if on cue, the elevator clunked and continued its upward climb.

The generator fed small emergency lights up and down the hall. As John stepped off the elevator, he checked the dim corridor. Lieutenant Davis sat at the monitoring station lit by the glow from the screens. They cast an eerie light on the young man. The two guards behind Lieutenant Davis studied John's form before relaxing.

"What happened to the power? Are all the computers back online?"

"Hospital criticals are. We have backup for our own critical systems. I'm tied into the utilities monitoring system. It looks like an overload for the whole city, but I don't have enough data to be sure yet."

"Keep me informed."

John walked past the door sentries. The soldiers in the hall had already hung electric lanterns throughout. Some visibly jumped when John walked past them. Others held their shotguns at the ready. The lanterns produced long shadows.

In the observation room, Keats sat still as Jason paced his room. Cross fidgeted in the corner.

"Something's going to happen," said Cross. "They know he's here, and they want him."

"Calm down, Cross. You'll give yourself a nervous breakdown," snapped Keats. "Any explanation about the lights, Colonel?" Keats's voice remained calm.

If the power outage bothered him, he did not show it.

"Looks like the power grid for the entire city overloaded. I understand it's not that uncommon this time of year."

Keats pointed to Jason. "If he were calmer, I'd be a great deal happier. Cross, why don't you go downstairs and get that blood sample from Ms. Touluc? My lab has power enough for most operations. You're like a nervous cat, and I find it distracting."

"I'd rather stay here," said Cross.

"Don't be such an ass, Cross ..."

John interrupted Keats. "It might be better if you wait till the lights come back on. I don't want people wandering around in the dark making everyone else nervous."

"Thank you, Colonel."

John felt less concerned with Cross than with how Avery and Clara would take to Cross being so nervous. While John would never admit it aloud, Keats's coolness acted as a stabilizer for him. It helped cool him.

"Have you tried talking to him again about the 'others'?" he asked Keats.

"I tried, but he won't say anything more than what he said earlier: 'They're coming for me tonight.' It's all I can get out of him."

"How does he know they're coming for him?"

"He won't say."

Jason stopped pacing and stared at the two-way mirror.

"What is it, Jason?"

Keats leaned forward, peering through the window expecting an immediate answer. Jason continued staring at the mirror, studying the men watching him.

"Is it like before?" Cross asked.

John and Keats both turned to Cross, surprised at the question. He had kept something from them both.

Cross continued, "Tell me, Jason?"

"Yes, but no. I can't be sure."

"What have you been holding back?"

John's sudden anger surprised Cross. Cross began talking as fast as he could.

"When he first got here, he said he felt peculiar, like when the others were near him in LA. I thought it was just wishful wanting on his part. Kids always want to find somebody like themselves. But then he got upset today, and those soldiers disappeared, well ..."

"It's got to be Touluc," said Keats, addressing no one in particular. "The only time he acts nervous is when she's in the building. He's calm when she's not here. They'll use her to get to Jason."

Before John answered, the lights flashed back on. They proved more blinding than comforting after so much darkness. Then they went out again.

"Get your syringe," he said to Keats. "We'll find out for sure. You stay here!" He growled at Cross.

Cross didn't move.

"I'm glad you're finally taking this seriously," said Keats as they walked out of the observation room.

"Don't get me wrong," John snarled. "I have people missing and have to take everything into consideration and Avery agreed to a new sample. Whatever you have against her, clear it up. I don't have time for the games you've been playing. If you've endangered any of my people because of these games, I'll have your ass out of the project before you know you're missing from it."

"A bit of bravado to stabilize the nerves? I thought you were above that, Colonel."

"Don't push me, Keats."

Keats said nothing but continued grinning.

They walked down the stairs to the eleventh floor. Avery's office was near the end of the hall. There were no critical systems on eleven. Only a few emergency lights guided them.

John held his flashlight to the floor. "Granton," shouted John. He didn't want to be shot. "Sergeant Granton," he shouted again.

He opened the door and gulped for air. Papers and files littered the floor, window glass was scattered everywhere, and the desk leaned against the wall. Clara lay among the papers on the floor. Before John could react, Keats bent over her with his hand to her throat. John grabbed his arm.

"I am a medical doctor."

John let go of his arm. Instinct now took control.

"Davis," he shouted into the radio, "I'm on eleven. Security's breached. Get Captain Black and his people here ASAP!"

"Yes, sir!"

Clara moaned sluggishly.

"She's only fainted," said Keats.

He opened the small medical bag he'd brought with him, took out a package of smelling salts, and handed it to John. Then he took out his blood draw equipment. He paused, putting a tourniquet on her arm.

"We need to be sure."

John nodded and lifted Clara's head. She waved her hand to move the smelling salts away from her face.

"I've never fainted a day in my life." Her words slurred out as consciousness returned. "Owww!"

She tried to jerk her arm away, but Keats held it steady.

"He's just taking some blood to make sure you're okay. Can you tell me what happened?"

Clara's mind began to clear. John helped her sit up. "Weird. I couldn't decide who was being the biggest ass — you or Avery. She just sat there at her damn computer." She noticed the tossed furniture and papers scattered about the room. "Oh, God, John, what happened? Where's Avery?"

"Let's get you somewhere to lie down. Slowly... Let us help you," said John.

He and Keats guided Clara off the floor, until they heard footsteps running down the hall. John handed Clara over to Keats and drew his pistol.

"Sir!" Captain Black had been running and gasped for air. Administrative work did not lead to good conditioning for running eleven flights of stairs. "There's no activity below. Twelve reports all quiet."

"What's going on, John?" A panicked clarity emerged in Clara's voice. "Where's Avery?"

"I want you to go upstairs with Dr. Keats. You'll be safe there. I'll find Avery. Captain, take two men and escort them."

"Yes, sir."

John thought Black sounded too relieved at not having to search.

"John?"

Clara wanted to protest but was still too weak to argue, and Keats and Black led her out of the room.

"All right, I want this floor checked out, room by room."

Before they could start, the lights flashed on only to flicker out just as quickly.

"Damn lights," whispered Sergeant Harris.

"Keep moving," said John.

Tension filled the air as John and five of his soldiers methodically searched the hall. Their flashlights and the small safety lights in the rooms gave the task an otherworldly atmosphere. They pushed the doors open, and kicked desks and tables out of their line of sight, but nothing gave any indication of what had happened or where Sergeant Granton and Avery might be.

The tension that had been building in John actually lessened as they reached the other end of the hall. Searching for something he knew, he did well. There was no sign of anyone. From the slow, breathy sighs around him, he could tell his men were also calming down and focusing on their purpose. They checked the door to the stairwell — locked. They began to walk back to the other end of the hall. The one room they hadn't looked in was the old nurse's station, although it could hardly be called a room. A counter separated an alcove in front of the elevators. Two half-walls met to make a niche where nurses used to fill prescriptions and gossip. He signaled Sergeant Harris and another to follow him. The cubicle sat empty except for Sergeant Granton, who lay stretched out on the floor with his throat ripped open. John stared, awed at how little blood had spilled on the floor.

Upstairs, the soldiers were visibly shaken as the news of Sergeant Granton's death spread. John moved automatically. He growled, and the soldiers straightened themselves. They carried Granton's body into the lab where Keats was examining Clara's blood. While his lab equipment was critical, lighting wasn't. Cross, sweating and fidgeting, prepared the center table to receive the body.

"She appears to be all right, Colonel. I left her on the couch in the coffee room." Keats barely looked up at John. "I'll know for certain when I'm done here. Then I'll examine Sergeant Granton."

"Thank you, Doctor."

John needed to see Clara. He had held his breath when entering the lab in case Keats had found the anomaly in her blood.

When John entered the coffee room, Clara lay on the couch. She jumped up and ran to John when he entered. He allowed himself only a moment with her. There was so much to do, and so many questions he couldn't answer.

"I heard them talking. You found that sergeant dead, didn't you?"

"Yes. We haven't found any trace of Avery."

"What's happening? I keep going over it in my head but…"

"It's going to be alright. Let me make sure that you're safe then I can find out for certain what's going on. Stay in here. If you need anything, if you notice anything alarming, call out. My people are right outside the door."

"Does this have anything to do with why you wanted Avery in here this evening?"

Clara insisted John give her some answers.

"I don't know. Tell me, what you do remember before you fainted?"

"I don't faint! Geez!" Clara looked off in the distance as though she was in Avery's office and remembered. "She wouldn't get off her computer. I walked to where she was sitting, intending to grab the keyboard away from her. That's when I saw the screen. She was looking into a room, more like a cell, at a boy with red hair pacing back and forth. It's just blank after that. I'm sorry."

"I'll tell you when we find Avery."

John left the room quickly. Clara had confirmed that Avery knew about Jason. The computer logs would tell him how long she had been plugged into the security system. *What was she playing at?*

Security sealed off the working wing of the twelfth floor. John moved to Davis and his monitors. The eleventh floor remained dark except for the red emergency lights. Most of twelve was dark, except in the rooms where night-viewing cameras were installed. Those monitors showed ghostly green-and-black shapes. The only rooms with movement were the lab and coffee room.

"Do you have what happened in Touluc's office?"

"I thought you might ask for that," replied Davis. "I kept a personal watch on them before the situation outside. Whatever happened in Ms. Toulac's office should have been recorded though."

"Good man. Show me."

John watched as Avery typed on her computer. Clara paced up and down the room. John fast-forwarded through most of it. He stopped when Clara began to get angry, and Avery stared out the window.

"Stop there," he said. "Is there something in the window?"

"They're eleven stories up. She must have been looking down where we don't have any cameras."

"Zoom in on the window." John was certain a shadow moved outside the window. He remembered the parking garage and the darkness inside of darkness. "She's looking straight out."

There was a beep from the control panel, and Lieutenant Davis looked at the other end of the monitor station. "Sir," he said, "someone's logged onto your computer."

"Avery," came out of his mouth before he realized it. "You two come with me."

The two guards behind him jumped and followed.

6

The hour being late, the night being Friday, the season being summer, the children sing in familiar unison to the beat of the latest tunes. The lights of the cars on the Seawall shatter the night with a reality that is not real. From the shadows in the middle of the street walk those who are never noticed. They stalk the gutters and congestion in hopes of a meal. And in the recesses of the mind's eye, another glides through the crowd, hungry.

> *When the tide is low*
> *and the sickle moon dances on the dunes,*
> *a new night begins where once*
> *there was only shadow.*
> *Do you feel it in the air, my children?*
> *The call for the tide is upon our lips.*
> *The night begins or ends with the Word.*
> *This is Mary Midnight at KMND Galveston.*
> *If you listen, you can hear what you want to hear.*
> *Speak the word and know your fear.*

Clara was tired, frightened, but bored. She was not meant to sit and wait. When she opened the door, she expected to be told to stay in the room. But the guards didn't seem to notice her.

Dr. Keats walked out of the room to her right. "Are you feeling better?"

Keats's solicitude surprised Clara. From Avery's descriptions, she'd expected to dislike him. Yet he had been very kind to her. He gently helped her up the stairs and stayed with her in the coffee room until she felt stable despite the fact he clearly wanted to be doing something else.

"Yes. Thank you. Is there anything I can do? I feel useless just sitting in here."

He considered a moment before answering, "Yes. You are involved now, I suppose. Come."

Before opening the door, he asked. "Do vet graduates learn anything about human anatomy?"

"I sat in on a few autopsies in school."

Clara knew before seeing it that they were entering the room where Sergeant Granton's body lay. Keats wanted her to assist while he examined the corpse.

She took a lab coat from a rack near the door. Keats spoke to a little man whom Clara guessed, going by Avery's description, was Cross. He left the room quickly with a look of profound relief. She walked up to the body and pulled the blanket off the sergeant's head. As she studied his wound, Keats moved to exam the wound from the other side of the body.

"You think Avery did this, don't you?" she asked.

John's behavior and Avery's disappearance were beginning to make sense.

"Yes," he said without showing any surprise at her question.

"It couldn't have been her."

"Why?"

Keats watched her face and saw that her declaration was the product of examination.

"Look here," she began, pointing to the closest edge of the gaping wound. "This is where the wound begins. Claws. Avery's nails are too long. They would have made a cleaner cut."

"Interesting."

"In my line, you get to know claws. I've had my share of run-ins with uncooperative patients. And you don't live in the same house with someone for fifteen years and not know something about her personal grooming habits."

Keats considered Clara's deduction and believed her. "What sort of animal did this?"

"Canine would have taken more flesh, bird would leave neater cuts. Perhaps human. I believe that would be more your expertise."

Before Keats could answer, they heard a gunshot. Keats rushed toward the door, turning back briefly to tell Clara to stay in the lab. Clara was faster and reached the door first.

"Oh, please," she said, rolling her eyes and opening the door.

There was confusion in the hall as some of the soldiers rushed toward the entrance and the others steadied their guns in that direction. Clara had decided it might be better in the lab when a loud "Clear!" sounded. It was John's voice. The lights flashed twice then came back on.

As her eyes adjusted to the light, she could make out the door to the other hall opening and John walking in hurriedly. He looked angry. Behind him came two men. Between them walked Avery, in handcuffs.

"What's going on? What were you shooting at?" Clara asked as soon as John came within easy earshot.

John's face turned gray when he saw Clara wearing a lab coat. He glared at Keats.

"She already knows some and guesses the rest. I didn't see any reason not to take advantage of her training. There's no one else here now who can help."

He added the final line for the benefit of Cross, who peeked through a crack in the door of the observation room.

"Never mind that," said Clara, looking first at John then at Avery with equal amounts of anger and suspicion. "What are you doing?"

"He's arresting me, Clara. I think that is obvious." Avery's sarcasm was too much for John.

"Take her in there," John said to Avery's guards. He then turned to Keats. "What do you think you're doing, getting Dr. Lucas involved?"

"Don't you dare start talking like I'm not here! If I wasn't involved before tonight, I am now. Accept it and move on!" She started to follow Avery until a guard stood in her way. "John!"

"Get your kit, Doctor," he said to Keats. "Come with me."

He took Clara by the arm and led her into another room.

"You have no idea what is going on here. I can't just let you wander into this blind. Let me have someone take you home."

Clara had thought she would never hear John plead for anything.

"It's too late, John. I don't know everything, but I suspect I know more than you want me to." She touched his face and tried to smile. "Let me help you. Whatever you think Avery's done, you know she'll talk to me."

John looked at her for a long moment. "We're all on edge. One of my men even took a shot at her in my office. She was just getting up from the desk. I like Avery, but I can't let this slide. She broke into my computer and accessed files; I don't know yet what damage she's done."

Without another word, he led Clara out of the office and into the coffee room. Avery sat at the table looking disinterested. The two guards who had taken her into the room remained inside the door watching.

"Your people aren't much for conversation tonight," she said as John and Clara entered. Keats followed them in. "If *he's* going to stay in here, I don't have anything to say."

"You're going to talk to me, and it doesn't matter who I want in this room."

John's voice was stern. Clara stood behind him. She was worried about Avery and knew, despite the tone, that John was too.

"You're tired, John? Why don't you get some sleep? We can talk..."

John cut her off. "I'll decide when we talk. What happened in your office, and what were you doing on my computer?"

She looked at Clara. "I didn't kill Granton."

"She's telling the truth. I saw the wound on the sergeant's body, and it couldn't have been her," said Clara.

"I agree." Keats sat down on the couch opposite Avery. "Dr. Lucas showed me that it couldn't have been Avery."

"But you know what happened." John never moved his gaze from Avery. "I want some answers."

"We all want answers. Problem is, we don't always get the ones we want. You certainly won't get any until I consult with my attorney."

"This is a matter of national security." John moved closer to Avery and bent over her. "You don't have any rights until I say you do."

"I'm not a scared little boy you can push around."

"Avery." The anxiety in Clara's voice was evident. "Tell him what he needs to know."

Avery smiled sympathetically at Clara. "You were there. Didn't you tell him?"

"I passed out. You know that."

Clara pleaded. Avery was always cool and aloof, but Clara had never seen her act so strangely.

"We can easily settle the matter," began Keats. "Let me take a sample of her blood. At least then we'll know exactly what we're dealing with."

"Over my dead body," Avery replied.

"If necessary," said John.

Avery's face went blank, as though she were thinking of something else.

"Do it, Avery," said Clara. "Let him take a sample and ..." Cross hurried into the room on the edge of panic.

"It's Jason!"

"Stay here," John ordered the two guards as he and Keats rushed out of the coffee room.

Clara followed them. When she entered the observation room, she saw the red-haired boy from the monitor in Avery's office. He was yelling, "Stop! Stop!" and pounding his fist against the walls. When he realized he was being watched, he turned his anger at the one-way mirror.

"You're killing me!" he shouted at them. "If you don't kill me, they will. Let me out!"

Keats turned on the microphone. "Jason." He intervened, but his voice only seemed to make the young man angrier. "Jason!" Keats shouted this time and turned on the sun lights. "Stop."

Jason screamed with pain as the lights beat down on him. He pulled the blanket off the bed and covered himself with it in the corner of the room.

"Make it stop!" His screams became whimpers.

"What are you doing to that boy?" Clara asked.

"Clara!" John turned toward Clara with surprise. "You shouldn't be in here."

"Is that what you have planned for Avery?"

"Put them in the room together," said Keats aloud to himself.

"What are you talking about?" John looked sharply at Keats.

"You know I'm right about her. Let her see what will happen if she doesn't cooperate."

"No!" shouted Clara.

"I want to know for sure."

Jason still whimpered in the corner of his cell, his madness nearly complete.

John went back into the coffee room. He wouldn't allow Clara to follow. She stayed in the hall just outside the door. She could hear Cross trying to calm Jason. She suddenly heard a loud "No!" from Avery and what sounded like furniture falling. John called, and two more soldiers entered the coffee room. A moment later one of the guards opened the door to leave. Clara could see John and the other three holding Avery against the wall. Keats pulled the needle out of her arm. There was a look in her eyes that Clara had never seen before.

"You'll pay for that one, Keats," Avery spat.

Keats emerged with a satisfied grin on his face.

"You shouldn't have seen that, Dr. Lucas." Keats paused in front of Clara. "I am sorry, but it had to be done."

Clara gauged that grin, coupled it with all that was happening, and knew that she no longer liked the man. John came out of the room next.

"Clara," he started, but she turned her back to him. He straightened himself up. "It took four of us to hold her. Why?"

John walked away without waiting for an answer.

Clara stood for a moment without moving. She didn't know what to do. She wanted to go to John and talk, but there were too many questions he wouldn't answer, and she was too angry not to get answers. The guards wouldn't let her talk to Avery. If she did get to see her, what could Avery say? Why did it take four grown men to hold her still? Did she kill the sergeant? And why hadn't Avery told her something so horrible was happening? These questions pounded in her head.

Cross's voice crept into her ear. She walked into the observation room and found him still trying to calm Jason. A bag of blood sat in the transfer box, but Jason ignored it. Cross looked up at her as she entered. He turned off the microphone.

"How is he doing?" she asked.

"He won't eat, and he won't talk. He's always talked to me. We're friends."

Cross looked pale and sweaty.

"Maybe I should try."

"He won't leave the corner."

"We'll see."

Her mind recalled the stories and myths she'd heard all her life from her mother and her grandmother. With all that she had seen, accepting myth for truth was the logical conclusion.

"Jason." She surprised herself at how calm her voice sounded. "I know you're hungry. I wish you'd take this. It will make you feel better."

Jason pulled the blanket off his head and looked to the mirror. "Who are you?"

"My name is Clara. You need to keep up your strength."

"Why?" Jason laughed. "I'm going to die and nobody gives a damn."

"I give a damn, Jason. My friend is in the next room. If you die, then so will she."

"Not her." He turned to look at the mirror and got up. He walked slowly to stand in front of Clara and put his hand up close to her. She put her hand on the glass against his. He looked directly at her then opened the box, took out the blood, and drank.

"Do you feel better now?" asked Clara.

She hadn't moved during the strange spectacle.

"Yes," he said, as he returned the bag to the box. "You want me to tell you about your friend, don't you?"

"What do you know?"

She no longer felt anxious about knowing the truth.

"She's like me, but not completely. I know when she's around, just like I know the others aren't far off. Sometimes she talks to me. In my head, you know. I'm not sorry about that sergeant. I didn't like him. He wasn't very nice to me."

"You know about the killing?" Cross asked.

"Yes. I'm sorry I didn't tell you about them or her sooner, Charlie." Jason turned back to Clara. "I can hear everything in the hall. You should go home. Something bad is going to happen."

"Something bad has already happened," Clara replied.

"Your friend is afraid, and not of Keats, and that makes me afraid," Jason concluded.

Clara walked out of the room, believing him. She also believed that if Avery was afraid, then she should be afraid.

Clara found John in front of the hall watching a replay of what had happened in Avery's office that evening. She could see and hear herself asking Avery about her monitor. She watched as her image walked behind the desk. Then the monitor went blank. Lieutenant Davis noticed her first. John followed his gaze.

"What's going to happen to Avery?" she asked.

"It all depends. At the very least she'll be charged with destroying government records. That's what she was doing on my computer. Even Davis can't find the files."

"And at the most she'll be put in a cell till she dies, like Jason."

"I don't know."

"May I speak with her?"

She could see John didn't believe the truth before him. The lights went off again.

"Damn it."

"It's the power grid again, sir."

The generators came back on and the emergency lights took up duty once more.

"John?"

"All right. But the guards stay."

Clara didn't object.

Avery sat with her eyes closed. She opened them when Clara walked in.

"I thought you might want to talk," said Clara.

She didn't know what Avery would tell her, but there *must* be something.

"What about?"

The little smile she always had still played on her lips despite the handcuffs.

Clara threw her arms up, tired of guessing and assuming. "I don't know. Like, how all this happened. What you're afraid of."

"What's happened that you don't understand?"

"Was it Max?"

Clara wanted someone to blame.

"No."

Avery looked up at the corner near the door. Clara followed her gaze and saw the camera.

"We are what we are, Clara. And you're my friend. Why don't you go home and get some rest?"

"I don't like being out in the witching hours. You know that. Tell me what you're afraid of."

Avery smiled warmly and tried to change the subject. "You've been talking to Jason."

"Damn it, Avery," Clara puffed.

"We're all afraid of something, Clara. The trick is to live with it. Why don't you get John to take you home?"

"He won't leave. Duty and all that shit!" Clara puffed.

"Duty, patriotism, glory, and faith. Isn't that what Victory says?" Avery paused. She looked intently at Clara and lost her smile. "Then there is nothing I can do for you, Clara."

Avery's countenance quickly changed. Before Clara could understand what was happening, Keats opened the door.

"My favorite person," remarked Avery, and the corners of her mouth resumed their upward stance.

"You're becoming *my* favorite person, Avery. Is there something you'd like to tell me?" His smugness filled the room.

"Yes," said Avery, "but not in mixed company."

"Your blood sample is very interesting. I think you and I are going to get to know each other very well."

He laid the medical box he had brought with him on the table and began to go through it.

"I don't think so."

Clara hardly recognized Avery. Avery glared at Keats with a look that told her she'd kill him given half a chance.

"Haven't we all had enough for one night?" Clara asked.

"It might be better if you left the room, Dr. Lucas."

Keats looked over at one of the guards and he stepped forward.

"Go on," said Avery. "It would be better if you left."

"I want to measure your fingernails," said Keats, as though Clara were already gone.

Clara ran to the end of the hall to find John. Avery was always level and calm. But the look she gave Keats horrified Clara. She found John still at the console in front of the hall.

"John," she said hurriedly, "you better come!"

He followed her at once. Before they could reach the coffee room, they heard a yell. One of the guards flew through the coffee-room door and hit the other side of the hall. The second guard walked backwards out of the room, shotgun aimed. John pushed Clara back and ran forward.

Avery came out of the room with Keats in front of her. One of her hands held tightly against his throat. His face was a deep shade of purple. The other hand held his arm behind him. She kept her back to the wall. The soldiers surrounded them, raising their shotguns. John raised his revolver.

"Let him go, Avery." His voice was solid and loud.

Clara gasped as Avery turned her head. It seemed to Clara that her eyes glowed red with the light of the electric lanterns.

"Tell them to back off, John, or I'll rip his throat out. You know I can do it."

Clara noticed the handcuff dangling on her wrist like a bracelet.

Avery moved steadily down the hall toward the window.

"I won't let you go," said John.

"You can't stop it."

Avery looked past John and saw Clara. She looked back to John. Keats gagged.

"Avery!"

Clara knew her plea would do no good, but she felt the need to try something.

There was a sudden crash and all eyes turned toward Clara. Jason ran into the corridor. He was cut and bloodied from smashing through the observation mirror. He slammed into Clara, knocking her to the ground. Clara looked up and cringed at his face, streaming with blood. His eyes burned like balls of fire in the lantern light. He screamed, and Clara could see sharp white teeth glistening at her. He started to bend over Clara, and then she heard a gunshot. The bullet went through his shoulder, but Jason barely flinched.

"Now."

Clara barely heard Avery's voice under the barrage of gunshots that followed and didn't know what she meant. Jason had turned but was soon on the ground. He huddled into a ball looking at Clara. His eyes looked like any boy's eyes would look. He was hurt and dying. He reached out to her, but he was dead. Most of the soldiers ran up to where he lay, their guns still smoking and pointed at the bloody mess they had created. John helped her up. She heard the sound of a single pistol shot. Clara turned to see that Avery had pushed Keats onto the floor. Captain Black stood against the wall opposite Avery, his pistol still in his hand.

Avery leaned against the wall holding her hands to her stomach. She slowly slid to the floor, leaving a trail of blood on the wall behind her.

John reached her first and helped ease her to the floor. "I'm sorry," he said.

"Why?" asked Avery, still smiling. "What did you expect when you hunt shadows?"

"Don't talk," said Clara. "It doesn't look that bad."

"Don't trust the dead, Clara." Avery's smile suddenly vanished, and she became very pale. "John," she said. "Get everybody out, now."

"What is it?" Clara asked.

Avery struggled to get up.

"Go!" Avery growled.

Clara had never heard anything like it before. The soldiers standing over Jason's body turned to face her.

"Get out!" roared through the hall like the wind. Avery turned her face to the window at the end of the hall. John grabbed Clara and began to run away from the window.

"Positions!" he shouted to the soldiers.

Clara felt that same chill run up her back that she had felt in Avery's office. John pushed her to the floor behind the line of soldiers. The electric lanterns went out all at once, and she heard the window crash open. There was gunfire and what sounded like a man crying out, then a loud screeching that reminded her of birds of prey, only mean, powerful, and angry. Then it was quiet.

Flashlights switched on. Sergeant Harris shouted a roll call. Capt. Black was missing. Clara realized she was practically on top of Jason's body. Her jeans were sticky with his blood. She got up and hurried to where she had left Avery, but Avery was gone. Clara put her hands over her mouth. She wanted to cry. John shouted orders, but she couldn't hear anything.

7

In an abandoned warehouse on Broadway, with a neon space monster painted on the outside wall, a radio is playing. A rat runs across a beam. A pale light comes through holes in the roof from the streetlights outside. A blanket is spread on the floor. Bottles and cans and condoms are scattered. Two long necks lie on their sides on the blanket, spilling golden juices. No one can be seen.

In the stillness before the dawn,
on an island in the mist,
in the land of shadows,
my children find their beds.
Dawn is not far off.
Do we know what it will bring?
I know what you find when you hunt for shadows.
This is Mary Midnight, at KMND Galveston.
The night is my realm.
Don't forget: You're only passing through on your way to the sun.

Someone made a fresh pot of coffee. John savored the aroma and took strength from the flavor. Since the attack, he had employed every ounce of his authority masterfully. He barked orders, he inspected, he made certain everyone saw him until order restored itself, and everyone performed the tasks he said they should be doing when he said they should be doing them. A small group still hammered plywood over the broken window. The broken glass, swept away and bagged for trash, waited only for someone to haul it away. Sergeant Harris, always strong and in control, led the small search party on the streets. Neither he nor John expected to find Captain Black or Avery.

John stood calmly listening to the melodies on the radio as they gave way to the soothing, seductive voice of the late-night DJ. John drifted away with that voice, which was both calming and alluring.

"Hunting shadows," he said to no one. "That's what Avery said."

He poured another mug of coffee and carried it to Clara in the makeshift triage area. He had watched her in the chaos that followed the attack. She wasted no time tending to anyone with an injury. The need for security made it impossible to use the hospital's emergency physicians and most of their own were off duty. Fortunately, minor cuts and bruises were the primary injuries. Keats and Cross would need professional attention; Keats for a bruised throat and Cross for a nervous breakdown. For now, quiet took over on the floor.

"I've done what I can do. Luckily, nothing serious," she said between sips of coffee.

"I imagine Keats will diagnose himself. At least I won't have to hear him tell me about it."

They tried to laugh but managed only smiles.

The sun peeked through the open blinds at the window.

Clara looked toward the light. "I'm going home."

"I'll get someone to take you."

"Thanks."

John placed his hand on her shoulder, wanting to be with her. "I can come by later."

"I want to be alone for a while. I need sleep."

"Call me if you need anything else."

John tried to hide the disappointment in his voice.

"Get some sleep yourself." She touched his face the way she always did, and the hurt disappeared. "Doctor's orders, and call me when you wake up."

She didn't ask about Avery.

She left as the replacements were arriving. Without his presence, there would be too much chatter and gossip. He remained in sight to keep minds on their tasks. Jason's body lay secured in the lab. He ordered two guards on the door until Keats examined it. Lieutenant Davis still worked at the security console.

"Where's your replacement?"

"On his way, sir. I'm just checking the system. Everything is operational now. Sergeant Harris reports nothing yet."

Davis seemed ready to plunge into more tasks when Lieutenant Ryan arrived.

"Make sure you get some rest." John wondered if he'd meant to say that to Davis or to himself. "Staff meeting in half an hour. Spread the word."

When the new guards were in place, the staff meeting was over, John saw everyone doing what needed to be done, and his notes for the reports he would have to write and file later were ready, he prepared for rest. He checked the hall once more. It looked much as it had the day before, except for the plywood over the window. Normality — he created it. The weekend crew meant fewer bodies to manage. Satisfied he had done as much as possible, John drove his motorcycle to the apartment. He barely had his shoes off before he fell into a deep asleep.

* * * * *

Shortly after four o'clock, Clara emerged from under the covers and pushed her toes into the loops of the carpet beside the bed. They both tickled toes and stimulated aching nerves. The sleep slowly eased out of tired muscles as she twisted and stretched. The window curtains were open and the bright sunlight reflected in from the heat on the beach. The sounds of the wind and the surf, and the air conditioner whining away in the summer heat comforted her in their normality. The bath-room door stood open, and the clothes she had thrown on the floor last night, the blood already dried black, reminded Clara too clearly of the last night's events.

Struggling to get out of bed, she stood. A slow growl from her stomach reminded her that she hadn't eaten since lunch the day before. In the bathroom, the blood-soaked clothes were beginning to smell. She put them in a plastic bag and tied it as tightly as possible. These clothes were beyond cleaning. The memories of last night were too strong. She tried not to look at them, but the image of Jason, bloodied and reaching out to her, remained in full color behind her eyelids. The growling stomach turned to a thud. She tried not to think about Avery. Perhaps she would be found, although the thought of Avery being found frightened Clara even more than her disappearance. If Avery showed up, Keats would find a way to keep her in a cell as he had with Jason. And John would have no choice but to do it.

In the kitchen, Clara poured water into the coffeemaker. She turned on the local news channel. *Inmate Attempts Escape from Prison wing of Sealy Hospital*, flashed across the bottom of the screen. That would be John's doing. That was probably why he had chosen the Sealy Hospital in the first place. The convicts would take the blame, and no one would question it. She thought about John bringing her that cup of coffee and wanting to be with her, and it made her smile. She'd wanted to be with John then. She wanted to be with John now. *Duty, honor, patriotism, faith. Why did he want victory so much? And victory over what?*

She wrapped her hands around a big mug of coffee and moved to the patio, picking up the phone along the way. She put it in the pocket of her oversized robe. *John would have stayed at the hospital most of the morning. He's probably still asleep.*

Curling up on the large chair in the shade, she watched the seagulls swirl and swoop in the warm gulf wind. Over the sound of the surf floated the chattering of tourists, teens playing loud music, and children laughing and crying and parents fussing and teasing. And through it all, she listened to the sound of the wind blowing around the houses and parked cars, and over whirling air conditioner units. The heat of the sun eased through her body, and she drifted back to sleep.

The phone rang. Startled awake, Clara hurriedly answered, hoping to hear John's voice.

"Clara?" asked her mother. "You sound like you've been asleep."

"Just taking a quick nap."

"One of these days you're goin' to have to settle down and stop stayin' out all night. You're missin' a perfectly lovely day."

Clara tried hard to say something.

"What's a matter with you, child? Are you goin' back to sleep on the phone? Put Avery on if you can't talk."

She hadn't counted on her mother calling her. "Avery's not here, Mama."

After a long silence, her mother asked, "What's wrong?"

"Nothing."

"There's somethin' wrong. I got ears. Do you want me to come over?"

"No!" Clara said quickly. The events of last night were only the start of something else. "Can I call you later?"

"That's okey, sugar. You call me when you're ready."

Her mother hung up. Clara relaxed, knowing she'd been reprieved. Mama knew when and when not to ask questions.

The clock on the microwave said six thirty. Clara realized she had fallen asleep on the patio. Her stomach growled even louder than when she had first woken up. She began to look through the refrigerator. A jar of spaghetti sauce sat at eye level, but the thought of spaghetti made her nauseous.

She heard a knock and started for the front door, but when the knocking resumed she realized it didn't come from the front door but from the patio door. Before she reached it, Max stepped into the living room. Clara saw only darkness as she fell to the floor.

The smell of eggs and shrimp and herbs woke Clara. Snapping and popping sounds came from the kitchen. Above her, the ceiling fan turned round and round. She started to sit up, but the room shifted under her. A large hand helped her sit up. Another helped her trembling hands grasp a glass of juice.

"Drink this. You need sugar first. Then I'll get you something to eat."

Max's voice rang as richly as she imagined it would, mellow with a peculiar mixture of accents, and surprisingly kind. Over the rim of her glass she watched him watching her. His wolfish eyes were sympathetic, and she noticed a little smile on the edge of his lips. It reminded her of Avery.

"Are you all right, now?"

She then realized that he was holding her up.

"Yes."

Despite his kindness, the image of Avery leaning against the wall with blood flowing out of her guts gripped in her mind. She blamed the creature before her for her friend's absence. She pulled herself away from him.

"Good. I'll finish your breakfast, then. I suppose we should call it dinner, considering the time, but I've never been too much of a stickler for formalities."

Max moved into the kitchen as though he always cooked there. He lifted a skillet off the stove and slid the contents onto a waiting plate.

"I've always liked playing chef," he began, "but don't get much occasion to do it."

From another skillet, he carefully lifted some large shrimp and placed them strategically around the omelet.

"Where's Avery?" She'd finally found the strength to speak. "And why am I on the couch?"

Max's little smile turned into a warm grin without quite extinguishing the wolfishness of his stare. "One thing at a time. You fainted." Before Clara responded, he continued, "Fight or flight syndrome. There's nothing you can do about it. It has nothing to do with being a weak or feeble female. Add to that not eating properly, too much excitement, and what do you expect? And then, of course, there's me showing up in your living room. I suppose I'm the last person you expected to see today."

She didn't want to like him, but something about him began to grow on her. "What's going on, Max? And why are you here now?"

She put her hand on her head. Her forehead beaded with sweat. Her respiration increased. She concentrated on her breathing to avoid fainting, again. Max placed the food on her lap.

"First, you need to eat," he said. "Then I'll tell you everything you want to know, assuming I have the answers you need."

Clara looked down at the plate. An omelet lay in the center framed with six large shrimp glistening from the steam rising slowly into her nose. Max had garnished the plate with thick lemon wedges. Carrots and spinach poked out of the omelet edges, tempting her. It looked like a photograph and the smells teased her nose. She looked at him again, suspicion edging its way to her face.

Max sat across from her. He leaned toward her, emphasizing his large frame over her small one. "If I wanted to kill you, I'd hardly resort to poisoning when there are more efficient and expedient measures available."

Hunger got the better of her, and she devoured the meal greedily. Max watched her every bite with interest.

When she finished, Max brought her a cup of coffee. His wolfish grin never faltered, and his eyes stared intently at her. Instead of his stare threatening her, his expression reminded her of her little nieces and nephews.

"It was very good. Thank you."

Max relaxed his shoulders as he took her plate into the kitchen and started washing dishes. Strength returned slowly to her limbs. Her head no longer wanted to float away, and the floors and walls remained fastened to the earth. She still kept her eye on Max. She didn't trust him, despite his culinary expertise, but she began to want to.

"I'm better now. Will you tell me what's going on? Where's Avery?"

Max came back to the chair opposite her. He studied her, determining her health and state of mind.

"And that captain? Where are they? Are they alive?"

"What do you know about me?" asked Max. "Aside from the fact that you don't like me."

"That you're the reason Avery is gone."

Since he knew she didn't like him, she decided pleasantries were unnecessary.

She didn't expect his answer. "It's better to say that I'm here because Avery is gone. She's not with me." He watched her reaction a moment then continued. "I was sent to Galveston to get Jason. I'd never even heard of Avery before I got here. She began to change before I arrived, but you already know that. As for your missing captain, he's not my concern."

Clara closed her eyes to remember details. Avery's behavior and habits had always been strange. Mama told her years ago that Avery didn't walk the same path they did. Until this moment, she didn't understand what mama meant. Avery's recent behavior began to make sense to her.

"She's helping you get to Jason. That's why you met last night outside the Bloodmobile."

"Yes, but nothing worked as planned. If I'm going to help her or Jason, I need you to tell me everything that happened. Tell me everything, even if you only think you know something."

He leaned forward anxiously.

"Jason's dead."

"A matter of interpretation, I suppose," said Max. "There's dead and then there's dead."

"Avery said not to trust the dead. Is that what she was talking about?"

Clara shivered a moment as she pictured her dying friend's final moment and the look on Captain Black's face as he stood back to the wall terrified that he had just killed a woman.

"Perhaps." Max leaned back in the chair, trying to conceal his impatience. "I can't be sure of anything until you tell me what happened."

"First, tell me who sent you and why you're here with me now. And I want to know who did this to Avery."

Her fear lessened as the food strengthened her body. A growing anger began to swell over her helplessness to understand everything happening around her.

Clara saw she had an advantage over Max. He needed information as much as she did. It did not escape her that Max might easily kill her, but his behavior did not register as threatening. Her anger fed her courage. She would insist on as much information as possible.

Max looked disappointed by her ultimatum but not surprised. He leaned back in the chair and put his hands behind his head.

"I'm here because Avery made me promise to protect you. She told me last night she couldn't hold off the change much longer and that Keats would easily discover that she'd switched blood samples. Despite all that, she insisted on going in to put the worm in the database. Once done, she'd make a distraction, I'd get to the twelfth floor and find Jason, and then we would all leave together. Very simple, really. But..." He paused, considering his next words carefully. "For now, I'll just say things didn't go as planned. As far as who did what to your friend, no one did anything to her. We're born vampires. That's not to say that everyone born a vampire will become one. Most never do.

"Never seen anyone like Avery though, in remarkable control of her change. But look, that's a long story that we don't have time for now. The sun will set in another hour, and she'll wake up." He again paused for a moment. "And she'll be hungry. If one of my kind has her, it will be okay. If your boyfriend has her... Well, let's just say it wouldn't be good for him."

The sternness with which he spoke the last part sent a shiver down Clara's spine. He didn't use that tone simply to frighten her. He needed her afraid.

The sun cast long shadows across the room. Max leaned back more in shadow than light, but his eyes caught burning embers of the sun and reflected them back in Clara's direction. His wolfish figure froze before her for an instant. *Avery and Max are so much alike.* Like Max's smile, Avery's little smile always carried a slightly sinister snarl. She always had a cold side.

Clara had asked her once why she had to walk the beach so late at night. "At night I feel so alive, like I could do something really terrible." Her old friend had left their world, but John remained in hers, and she would protect him even if he didn't know he needed her protection.

"It started at the parish hall," she began to tell Max all he needed to know.

Max listened intently. He leaned forward and questioned her in detail. At other times he just listened. He became excited when she described seeing a figure standing beside Victory on their way back to the hospital but didn't explain who he thought it was. When Clara reached the end of her story, Max grew visibly paler, if possible considering the pallidness of his skin. He stood up, began to pace around the room, then stopped for a moment in front of the patio doors. The blue sky deepened, and the reds and purples of night started to appear on the distant horizon.

"Not good," he said, more to himself than to Clara. "Why didn't he tell me? Too many involved in all of this."

"I've told you what happened," said Clara. She didn't like Max's reaction or his quiet mutterings. "Now you tell me your story. What is it that's worrying you?"

Max slowly turned and walked around the room again. He stopped to look at her as though he was about to speak, and then he paced some more.

Staring out the windows once again, he said, "If I had found him early enough, I might have helped Jason. He's too young for the change. I told you, we're born this way. Symptoms of change may show up in puberty, but most will never make the change. They resist the change and go on to live ordinary lives. From what I gathered, he was like any other street kid you see in any city. Most of us started out that way. Few claim to remember any real parents. So, it's not surprising that's where he was found. He got messed up with that Cross fellow. I've seen them together. He genuinely cares about Jason, might even be in love with him. He got Jason involved in Keats's blood study, so he'd have a few hot meals. But that's when it went all wrong."

"If you've been watching him all this time, why did you let Keats get to him?" Clara interrupted.

"I haven't been watching him all this time. Some things I've been told, some facts I've deduced, and others I supposed. No idea why Jason left Cross's care. I speculate: his were senses already beginning to sharpen and warned him not to trust Keats. Whatever the reason, after he left Cross, Thomas found him. He and his bunch love it out in LA with all the beautiful people. They fit right in. Bloody pricks!"

"Thomas?"

"Little cherub of a grocery clerk. You've met him."

"Son of a bitch!" Clara burst out.

Max paused as the news of sweet little Tommy being a vampire settled in.

"Like I said, too many involved." He continued, "Obviously, Thomas made his change when he was very young, but back in the day, who wouldn't? No one lived terribly long, especially street urchins. Unfortunately, he still acts like a little prick. Most of us call it bad form to encourage kids to make the change. They never really fit afterwards and sort of wither away."

"I invited him into this house." Clara's voice rose several octaves. "I let him use the phone. Hell, I even gave him a flashlight to make sure he'd be okay."

Max poured Clara another cup of coffee. "Drink this. You're getting excited. That won't do if you're going to help your friends. You need to gather your strength."

Clara closed her eyes and composed herself. "You're right. Please, go on."

"Thomas wanted Jason to make the change and become one of his toadies. Personally, I wouldn't have thought Thomas would be interested in Jason. I mean, he's not particularly pretty. Oh well, he ended up scaring Jason half out of his wits. Jason became convinced that Thomas would kill him. He's a bit off in the head, if you haven't noticed, so he ran. Of course, the physical changes and urges were becoming more pronounced. Naturally, he ran straight to Cross. And Cross, of course, took him straight to Keats. This I know because Thomas told me."

"That night I saw you two at the grocery store!" exclaimed Clara as the parts of the story began to make sense to her.

"No. Afraid that night you saw us together had nothing to do with Jason. I wanted to warn him off Avery and you."

"Why?"

"She has a very powerful friend protecting her. The little shit thinks he knows best."

Clara's eyes widened, and she was about to ask who the friend was when Max lifted his hand.

"Please don't ask. It's better that way. If I frightened you, he'd have you pissing your panties. Hell, without his blessing, I wouldn't have gone anywhere near Avery."

The look of fear that passed over Max's face startled Clara. She let it sink in that Avery had someone scarier than Max protecting her.

"Back to how you came upon Jason and all of this."

"The myths about us are only myths. We encourage them when we can for our own protection. After all, you are a bloodthirsty group. Most of us actually only live short lives. It's a hard way to live, so when an old one comes around, you do what they say. They know more secrets and are more powerful than you can imagine." Max stopped talking and started outside for a while. "A certain one called me to Los Angeles. He had heard of some trouble there involving Thomas. You can imagine Thomas getting royally pissed that I showed up. But when I told him who sent me, he stood aside. It took a while, but I found Jason. He already trusted Cross, and let's face it, my face doesn't do a lot to instill trust in people. Keats hadn't gotten the government involved yet, so I didn't have trouble talking to him. Nearly had him convinced to come with me when Thomas barged in. Afraid I indulged myself a bit in beating the shit out of Thomas. In the process, Jason ran off. Before I managed to get back to him, Keats had him in lock and key. It all went bad from there."

"You were called out for failing. Weren't you?"

Clara watched anger and fear cross his face at the same time.

"I lost Jason before the New Year. By March I had given up finding him. That's when the old one showed up. Both Thomas and I did a lot of squirming to stay alive. Of course, the old one found Jason quick enough. Problem is, Jason's senses were getting sharper. He felt our presence and told Cross. We didn't have time to get to him." Max stopped talking for a moment as though he suddenly realized something important. "Avery must have told him Jason would come here. Damn! She's good. Anyway, he sent me straight out here to scout things out."

"How did Avery know?"

"They've been friends for some time. Why didn't I put it together sooner? He's grooming ... never mind. What's important for you right now is that it's her time. He'll have her. He's the only one who could have taken her the way you described it. I need to make sure you're safe tonight. I'll worry about Jason tomorrow."

Clara accepted everything Max was telling her. Everything that had happened made sense when she did. "It's the old one's presence that I felt at the hospital last night."

"You're good. Must be all this time living here with Avery. But be careful who you say that to." He waited for his warning to sink in. "They're not keen on anyone knowing about them. After exposing himself so much last night, he'll be particularly keen to remain hidden. That could be a problem for you, but that's how they survive for so long.

"Anyway, about last night ... Thomas and his lot were waiting for me at the hospital. We planned to get both Jason and her out of there. They created the scene in front of the hospital. He may be an ass, but he'll do what needs doing. The distraction allowed me to get onto twelve unabated."

"Did you kill Sergeant Granton?"

"No." The surprise on Clara's face made him wait a moment before going on. "That only caused security to tighten up. Besides, no one leaves bodies lying around. Very sloppy. Had Avery done it, she would have reacted differently to being shot and certainly wouldn't have allowed herself to be arrested."

Clara sighed, relieved and worried by Max's answer.

"Avery's friend," Clara spoke slowly. "I mean, with her change? Leaving a body would be like a calling card, wouldn't it? You, Tommy, and his friends would stay away?"

She didn't need Max to answer.

Max continued with his story. "I tried to get to Jason. His mind's totally snapped now. Not anything there left to reason with. The closer I got to him, the more nutty rantings. At least he caused enough distraction for me to get out of the hospital. I tried to hook up with Thomas to get Avery, but they were all gone."

Max stopped. Clara realized he would say little more about what happened. She moved on to a new fear steadily growing in her mind.

"Avery's been shot, perhaps badly enough to kill her. Would that stop her change?"

"No. It would be easy enough to keep her alive, but when she wakes up, she'll be hungry."

"When will she wake up?"

Max shrugged. "I don't know. The first hunger is all-consuming. Her injury will make it even more so. That's why I'm here. She'd kill you if she were here. She'd regret it later, but she would do it."

Clara saw no reason to doubt him. "Jason's not dead. He'll wake up soon, won't he?"

"Yes."

"And he'll be hungry."

"Yes."

"I have to warn John." She stood up. The thought of Jason waking, and John being there made her shudder. "He'll kill anyone he sees."

"There's nothing you can do. If you warn your boyfriend, he'll want to know how you came by your information. Even then, he won't believe you. Despite what's happened, you're asking a very logical man, an experienced soldier trained to battle enemies, to accept the existence of monsters. We survive because people don't want to admit we exist despite what they see in front of them. I only promised to protect you."

"But he will listen to me. He loves me."

Clara smiled as she spoke. She realized for the first time how much she loved him. She started for the stairs that led to the bedrooms.

"I can't protect you if you leave here."

"Fine." Possible arguments she could use with John were already forming in her mind. She shouted over her shoulder to Max, "You don't have to go with me, but you'll answer to Avery if anything happens to me."

Clara remembered the look in Avery's eyes when Keats spoke. Avery always had that fuse in her and the capability to manipulate it. Now she had the capability to use it in a deadly manner. Avery and Clara had been friends too long for Clara to be threatened by her.

The cell phone slipped out of her pocket as she pulled off her robe. The battery light flashed and blinked out.

"Shit," she said under her breath.

She picked up the landline and dialed John's cell phone. Nothing. She dashed back to the living room. Max was gone. She picked up the land line and dialed John's cell phone. Voice mail answered.

"I guess you're still asleep or haven't turned the ringer back on your phone. I'm leaving for the hospital now. Please, don't go near Jason or let anyone near him till I get there."

Clara promised herself to plug in her cell phone every night.

Next, she dialed John's office number. Lieutenant Ryan picked up the line.

"No, ma'am. The colonel is currently unavailable," said Lieutenant Ryan.

"Tell him I'm coming there and ..." She stopped and thought better of leaving a message. "Never mind, I'll tell him myself."

She took a deep breath to calm herself. Carefully, she turned out the lights and locked the doors. Outside, she opened the storage area below the house. In a large wooden crate were souvenirs from her family's past that she had gathered over the years, including the old machete her grandfather had used to cut sugar cane. She liked to keep these treasures in good shape. The blade and wooden handle were regularly oiled and cleaned. The edge of the blade refracted the small overhead light of the shed. She wrapped the knife in an old beach towel and put it in her overly large beach bag she sometimes used as a purse. Avery's jeep worked better than her car, but she hated driving a standard. Tonight, she needed efficiency, so she took the jeep. With a deep breath, she started the engine and drove onto the road.

8

The shadows of the setting sun fade to night. Summer's heat rises from the sand, shimmering through the tall grass waving in the summer breeze. Night falls early on the island. A greenish light stretches into the approaching darkness from the open door of a cinder-block building. The sea breeze caresses the shore. A cat purrs in warm sand. The letters above the door flash in blue neon *KMND*. The door closes. Wings flutter in the distance as a voice on the airwaves whispers, and the night envelops all.

It begins again.
Somewhere is the truth,
the truth that is
and the truth that is a myth.
Tonight, my children, Victory stands waiting.
Follow me to the laurel crown.
You're listening to KMND Galveston.
I'm Mary Midnight.
When all the pomp is set aside,
the truth can be a dreary thing.
Be careful what you seek
in case it finds you.

Kate had done three tours in Iraq and never fired a gun. They married. She delivered two healthy children with a midwife at home and cooked dinner the next day. He promised, "Just one more assignment with Colonel Espinoza, and I can retire without worrying about being called up later." Kate had agreed. She had a good head on her shoulders, and her father would make certain his grandchildren wanted for nothing. She'll be okay.

He regretted that he would not see his kids graduate high school and go to college, and that he would not be able to attend the school plays or help them with homework. All this because he agreed to one more assignment.

Colonel Espinoza demanded the best, and Captain Black always gave it to him. Sure, the colonel didn't like it when he showed up with forms for signing and schedules to complete, but his efficiency allowed the colonel time to focus on the assignment. Despite seeing Jason and all the evidence he had heard Dr. Keats talk about, he hadn't believed in vampires. *Of course, I do now.*

Captain Black looked again at the growing shadows. The sunlight spilling in through the gaps in the boards that used to be windows shortened. Night would be here soon. He tried to reposition himself. Whoever tied his hands behind him had done a good job. He could sit up, but no more than that. The rope was tied to something on the floor behind him. He leaned against the dusty post in an old warehouse. Empty bottles and trash littered the dirty floor. In the heat of the afternoon, he had smelled stale cigarette smoke, alcohol, and marijuana. He hoped that whoever made the trash in here would come back before the sun went down and help him, but he doubted anyone would.

What would Colonel Espinoza tell Kate? Captain Black died in the line of duty? Is this in the line of duty?

"Is anyone looking for me?" he wondered out loud.

He looked again at the body lying ten feet from him. Whatever had pulled him from the hospital and knocked him out had been very careful with her. She lay on a smooth, cozy blanket, her arms neatly folded on her chest. If not for the huge bloodstain on her shirt, anyone would think she simply slept. Even in death, she was a beautiful woman. *She is something!* Captain Black had never shot his pistol at anyone. He never expected to. *What are the odds that the one person I would shoot would be a beautiful woman who turned out to be a fucking vampire?*

He wanted to laugh, but the light continued fading. He would be dead soon. No one would find his body. No one would know exactly what happened to him. Well, he would.

"And her," he said to no one.

He looked at her again. Her eyes opened. They were the last thing he saw.

* * * * *

John slept better than he had in days. If he dreamed, he didn't remember the details. He was grateful for that. During the day, there were no shadows moving across the walls or hiding in the trees to make him jump. He sat at his desk fully alert and ready to face whatever the new night had to offer. Several times he picked up the phone to call Clara, but hesitated. He had called before he left the apartment but got no answer. He hoped she was with her family, but he doubted it.

The shadows on the walls of his small office stretched long and thin as evening faded away. He turned to look out the window. He could look over the hospital campus and over the historic district to the ships at the docks. Just enough daylight remained for him to see beyond the ships to Pelican Island and the A&M campus. Past that island, on the mainland, the chemical plants along the coast began to light up like a great city.

Clara didn't like the view from his office. She told him she preferred the one from Avery's. Her office looked over the Seawall and beach and out to the Gulf. John admitted to envying Avery's view, the vast expanse of sky and sea melding slowly into one imagination.

He picked up the phone to call Clara again but stopped. The line between his professional concern and his emotional attachment to her crumbled. If he didn't talk to her, he wouldn't insist on explanations he didn't want to hear. Clara reacted in surprise at Avery's arrest but not at Avery's behavior. She spoke to Jason, even gave him a bag of blood without any prompting. *How did she know what he was?*

Facts began to come together in his head. He shuffled through the papers until he found Lieutenant Davis's report. Avery had almost managed to wipe out their entire database apparently trying erase all evidence of Jason's existence. The first attack had given Avery the time she needed to work and possibly allowed someone else access to the floor. The final attack had been specific. It got Avery out but not Jason.

John stood up and pressed the intercom to call Lieutenant Davis when Clara walked into his office.

"I was just getting ready to —"

Clara cut him off. "We have to talk."

"Yes, we do."

"Where's Jason?"

John sat back in his chair. "Jason's dead," he said. "Keats looked over him earlier. There's nothing to worry about."

Clara sat in the chair in front of the desk and put the large purse she sometimes carried in her lap. "He's not dead, John."

The seriousness of her face impressed John enough to consider the possibility.

"What makes you say that?"

"Don't patronize. It doesn't suit you." Despite the coolness of her expression, her voice betrayed anxiety.

"I took a look at him myself, Clara. There wasn't that much left of him to look at. He's *dead.*"

He expected her to get angry; instead, Clara sighed and leaned back in the chair.

Finally, she said, "Show him to me. Let me see for myself."

"Will you tell me about last night?"

"You were there."

"But you know more than I do."

Clara bit her lip and smiled. "I can tell you with confidence that Jason isn't dead. He'll wake up soon, and someone on this floor will die. Take me to him, please."

"Okay, but then we talk."

Clara smiled and stood up eagerly. "I promise."

The guards stationed throughout the lab hall had electric lanterns out and ready in case the power failed again. Guards and lanterns had doubled their numbers since last night. The tension rising as the dusk turned to night wreathed through the quiet of the floor. John eyed the plywood at the far end of the hall. As they approached the door to the lab, Keats emerged, looking perturbed.

"If you're going to change security on me, Colonel, I wish you'd inform me instead of letting me waste my time." Even in a coarse whisper, he sounded self-righteous.

"I thought you were going to rest."

"I'm the best judge of my own health. Where did you put Jason?"

"What do you mean?"

"I mean, where did you put the body? I need to do a full autopsy."

John pushed Keats aside and walked into the lab. The windows remained sealed and unbroken. There was no other door to the room. The sheets that had covered the body were still on the table and bloodied.

"We're too late," said Clara who had followed John inside.

"Not now, Clara. Sergeant!" yelled John. "Who took the body out of here?"

Sergeant Harris stared at the table, eyes widening. "No one, sir. Dr. Keats has been the only person in or out of the room since you ordered it off limits."

"I want all exits covered. Put a search team together."

"Yes, sir," snapped the sergeant.

Before he could leave, John stopped him. "And Harris, take two and go down to the morgue. Make sure Granton is still there. If he is, set a guard. Whoever took this body is trying to get all our evidence."

Harris's face went from shock to disgust then back to sergeant in a flash.

John looked at Clara. "The body must have been taken, Clara. They tried to wipe out any trace of the project last night. They're back."

"And just how did they get in here and do that?"

Clara's pallor fooled John for a moment. Anger flushed her face.

He pointed to the grid on the air duct hanging open in the ceiling. "Up there."

"He'll try to get out of the building," she said.

John ignored her last comment. "Come with me. You too, Keats."

He took Clara by the arm. Keats began to object but a firm "Now!" silenced him. John led them to the front hall. Activity bustled as a search began. Soldiers kicked open doors and turned on lights in every room.

"Air vents!" shouted John, but grates were already being pulled open.

At last they reached the end of the hall and the monitoring station. "Why wasn't that room monitored?" asked John to Lieutenant Davis.

"Didn't expect to need to monitor a corpse," said Davis, adding a belated, "sir."

John sat Clara down behind the lieutenant. "I want you to stay here. Don't go anywhere."

"But, John..." she started.

"Stay. I can't do my job if I'm worrying about you."

Clara sat down. "That's the nicest thing you've ever said to me."

"And you." John looked at Keats. "Stay out of the way."

Keats made no reply while absently rubbing his throat.

"Keep them here," he said to Lieutenant Davis. "An open attack would have happened by now before the full shift change. Whoever took the body is simply trying to get it out."

"Yes, sir." Lieutenant Davis never took his eyes off the monitors. "Sir, one of the elevator alarms just went off. The alarm is between two and three, but the car is up on five."

"Move!" shouted John.

He and four soldiers ran down the hall and started down the stairs. John halted after three flights. The others stood still, listening.

"Nothing," he said.

"Sir?" asked the square soldier with thick glasses.

She tightened the grip on her gun.

"No one heard or saw anything. Why would an alarm go off on the way down and not on the way up? Brown, Candida. Take this floor to the other end and come up the other stairs. Make sure the door is still locked. I want it covered, and try not to shoot any patients or staff."

As his mind began to race, the thought of accidents seeped in. The accidental shooting of any patient or staff member now would give someone the distraction they would need to move around with ease.

"You two come with me. Signal Harris to check out the elevator shaft."

He quickly turned, taking the stairs two at a time.

"You think they're still on the floor?"

Checkers, the red-headed corporal scanned the corners of the stairwell. Vargus, one of the largest soldiers in the company, looked down the next flight.

"Could be. They didn't need the elevators or the stairs last night," John said.

He didn't say that Clara had given in too easily to his command to stay with Lieutenant Davis, or that Clara knew more about what was going on than she was saying. With everything he had seen, what if Clara was right?

He hurried to the monitoring station. Lieutenant Davis flashed images across the screens before him. Clara still sat in the chair clutching her purse. Keats still stood behind her looking bored.

"I want every room monitored. They may still be on this floor." He turned to Clara. "If you have anything to tell me, it should be now."

Before Clara could speak, the elevator door opened. John and Davis hurriedly pulled out their weapons. The two guards on the door behind them lowered theirs. Checkers and Vargus moved forward. Even Keats stood at attention. The doors stood open for a moment then the bell rang and the doors closed. Everyone breathed again.

"Davis," John started, expecting him to have found something in the monitors by now.

"Nothing, sir. I can watch the mice sitting under desks but that's it. There's nobody there."

"Concentrate on movement," said Clara calmly. She looked directly at John. "The dead don't produce body heat. Your sensors wouldn't be able to pick them up."

"Suppose she's right," said Keats in his hoarse whisper. "After all, we've been through, Colonel, I'm surprised you still have doubts. Nothing in my research suggests he shouldn't still be dead and laid out in my lab, but as myths are clearly being turned around, I think you should consider the possibility that Jason is alive."

"I'm accepting nothing —"

"Sir," interrupted Lieutenant Davis, "I have movement."

John hurriedly got behind Lieutenant Davis and watched the monitor. "Show me."

A live map of the lab wing, including ductwork and maintenance shafts, lit up on the screen. A blur on the screen moved its way to the monitoring station. "That's it," said Davis, pointing to the blur. "Too big for a mouse, and it's coming our way."

"In the air vent?"

"An access shaft just above."

The blur on the screen grew closer. Suddenly it vanished.

"What happened, Davis?"

John motioned the two guards on the door to get ready, but they were already studying the ceiling above them.

"Could be a passage we don't know about." A movement blurred its way on the other side of the screen. "There he is. Must have moved through an area we don't have monitored."

John rushed out of the lab wing with Checkers and Verges following. They fanned down the administration corridor. Gunshots sounded in the stairway at the far end of the office wing. They ran down to the other end. Remembering the two he had sent to these stairs earlier, John ordered no one to shoot. There were enough corpses already.

By the time they reached the far end of the hall, the shooting had stopped. They could all smell the gun smoke and see the faint wisps of gray in the staircase.

Checkers reached the stairwell first and led the way. "Down here!" he shouted.

He held up a shotgun, recently fired. Spent shell casings littered the stairs along with a pair of regulation glasses broken in two.

"Brown or Candida," he shouted.

No one responded.

John felt anger beginning to take control of him. He had kept it in check long enough. "I want this hall and this stairway searched. You two come with me."

They were halfway down the hall when they heard the scream. It was decidedly female and decidedly Clara's. Three gunshots from a revolver and one shotgun blast followed the scream. John raced ahead of the others, his heart beating faster than it ever had.

John ran too fast and had to slide to stop. Lieutenant Davis lay against an elevator door, gun in hand. He shook his head, stunned from being thrown against the door. In the center of the floor, Jason leaned over one of the guards. John's nightmares came back to him as Jason's mouth pulled away from the soldier's neck. The neck held a gaping red wound, but little blood spilled onto the floor. Another guard lay in front of the desk, his throat torn, his face a deadly pale.

Keats pressed against the wall behind the desk frozen. Clara pulled herself up off the floor. Jason hissed at John. The only remaining trace of the blood and gore from the previous night were on Jason's clothes. Fresh blood surrounded his mouth.

Jason followed John's eyes across the hall to Clara. The others arrived, weapons at ready, but John held up his hand to stay them.

"Hello, Jason." Clara's voice sounded calm despite the sweat forming on her brow. "Do you remember me?"

John caught her gaze and tried to hold it as the soldiers spread out around him.

"You were nice to me. I remember," he hissed and turned back to John.

The soldiers took a step back.

"Jason," said Clara. "I can still help you if you let me."

Jason turned back to Clara and looked questioningly.

"I understand what's happening to you," Clara continued. "Let me help you."

"No one can help me!" he shouted back to her. He pointed an accusing finger at Keats. "He did this to me!"

"You asked for my help." Keats managed slightly more than the coarse whisper. "I can still help you."

"Liar! You're going to let them hurt me."

Child's tears streamed down Jason's face. Clara saw the child's face with fears no adult should have.

"I won't let that happen, Jason." Clara spoke quickly, smoothly. "Let me help you."

Jason's tears ran faster, washing the blood away from his lips. "No one can help me. I'm a monster. That's what I'll always be."

He looked down at the soldier he had just killed.

"He tried to kill you. You had no choice."

"I had a choice," he said, "but they wouldn't let me go."

John tried to move closer to Jason, but this only made Jason move closer to Clara. Clara held her ground, neither backing away from Jason nor reaching out to him. She clutched at the oversized purse as though it would protect her. John suddenly noticed that as she clung to the bag, she was also opening it. He expected the contents to spill out at any time to act as a distraction.

Clara smiled with certainty. "But you don't have to be a monster. You know I'm telling the truth."

"It's too late. They all want me dead. I just want to be left alone."

Jason stopped moving and studied Clara. He seemed calmer. He suddenly grabbed his head with both hands. "Stop it! You want me dead, too!" he shouted as loud as he could.

Keats leaned forward but remained against the wall. "Now, Colonel! Shoot him."

"No," yelled Clara to John. "Jason, I want to help you."

"Make them stay out of my head. Why won't they leave me alone?"

Jason flashed monster and child and monster. John aimed his pistol.

A single gunshot blared from John's right. Lieutenant Davis had managed to recover. The bullet pierced Jason's side, but Jason only flinched. He turned away from Clara and growled at the lieutenant. Before Jason could lunge at the lieutenant still on the ground, metal sliced through the air and Jason's head rolled toward the elevators. Davis jumped quickly to his feet, away from the rolling object. Jason's body fell, quivered, and shook before it finally stilled. John stared, amazed at how little blood oozed out of the open neck.

Clara walked over to Jason's head, the machete still in her hand and knelt down staring at the face. John knelt beside her and looked too.

"Mama always said, 'To make sure they're dead, cut off the head,' but I always thought she was talking about snakes."

Clara seemed mesmerized by the boyish face that stared back at her. Even John could recognize no sign of the monster or murderer or madman, just a freckle-faced teenager whose only worry should have been a date for the prom. John reached out his arm and helped Clara up. He wasn't even embarrassed as he held her close, and she clasped her arms around him.

Clara knew she would never forget the sight of Jason's face staring up at her. Those clear eyes, the pale lips open in a perpetual scream. They would always haunt her. She found herself suddenly thinking of Bela, that big dog with the brown eyes who always cried when Miguel held him down for her to examine. But Bela always wagged his tail happily as he walked out of her office. He might cry, but he remained sane. Jason had been mad. Max had told her how his mind had cracked in the captivity and confusion he'd been subjected to by Keats. He might have lived a long life.

She became conscious of John's arms around her and the sounds of the soldiers moving up and down the hall, still searching for anything that didn't belong. John didn't like such displays of affection and she pulled herself away.

"I'm okay," she told him.

He kept one arm around her and began to lead her out of the entry hall.

The bustle of movement and sound around her made it difficult for Clara to focus on anything. She concentrated on the door to the lab wing. She had a strong desire to be alone with John and just sit somewhere quietly. A man moved past the corner of her eye. His familiar form caused her to turn her head toward him. He pushed a gurney to the body of Jason, and like a giant predator he bent over and scooped it up to the gurney. Clara ignored the whole process and turned back to the front. She wanted to remember the boy she had tried to help.

"Get it to the lab and lock it up," said Sergeant Harris.

"Yes, Sergeant," replied the man.

That voice! She looked back quickly. Two men push the gurney into Keats' lab. The man with the voice turned to face her just as the door closed. His hair was cut in regulation style, but it was definitely Max. He took off his cap and winked as John led her through the door to the administration wing.

*****

Clara sat down on the couch in the break room. "I'm okay. Really. It's not like I've never put down a sick animal."

John poured a cup of coffee and handed it to her. "You weren't putting down one of your dogs. Jason was a kid."

"A kid I witnessed killing Lewis and Carroll, men I spoke to almost daily since you arrived."

John studied her face for a moment then bent down and gave her a kiss. "All right. Stay in here. I need to see to things."

He turned to walk out.

Clara wanted to tell him about Max. She hated herself for not telling him earlier, but she wanted John to survive. That meant Max had to get rid of the evidence. His kind survived because no one wanted to know they existed. Still, John deserved to know the truth.

"John," she started, but Keats walked in.

"Lieutenant Davis is fine. He'll probably have a hell of a headache. Is there anything I can do here?"

"We're good here. I'd appreciate it if you stayed in this room with Dr. Lucas."

"Of course."

"Clara?" asked John.

He turned back to face her.

"Later."

John stared at her a moment. He could tell she wanted to say something but didn't press for details. Clara sat down on the couch and sipped coffee.

"Looks like we're about out," said Keats as he poured a cup for himself. "I'll make another pot. I imagine we'll need it tonight."

He continued with the small talk, but Clara didn't listen. She wondered about the other man in the lab with Max — would Max kill him, wound him? She hoped the man would be safe and hoped Keats would stop rambling. His small talk annoyed her more tonight than in the past.

She turned her attention back to her companion. Keats watched her with the skill of a researcher. He understood her need for distraction. Now, he considered if she needed rest instead.

"I can get you a sedative. You look as if you need it."

"No," she said. "It's just a lot to take in. Sorry if I'm not much company."

"I'd rather your company than theirs." He motioned to the door leading to the hall.

"How's Dr. Cross?"

She wanted to keep control of the conversation. She didn't like Keats, but he had the annoying habit of being nice to her.

"Heavily sedated," he answered. "He took it personally when Jason snapped. I believe he was genuinely fond of the boy. Then seeing him put down like that — well, I don't suppose he'll be of much use to me anymore. A good assistant is hard to come by."

Clara sneered a little. "So, you're just going to write him off."

"Of course not." Keats looked offended. "I'm overseeing his care my-self. He knows too much to let just anyone else near him."

Though she tried, Clara could find neither compassion nor in-difference in Keats' expression. Cross transferred from colleague to patient for Keats, a task to deal with in a certain way. She realized he functioned scientifically, without room for attachment or compassion. Clara suddenly felt sorry for him. The detachment he effused was the same defense mechanism she felt when she had to euthanize her patients. But at the end of the day, Clara let the emotions pour through her and strengthen her. That was what made her a good vet.

She was recovering from a version of that detachment now. As soon as she'd made up her mind to take the machete out of storage and use it to kill Jason, her professional detachment had enveloped her. Logic drove her. She killed Jason or Jason would kill John. The difference between her and Keats was that Clara understood that when the crisis was over, she would deal with the emotions; she would cry for Jason, the boy caught up in a dangerous power struggle. Her family and John would remind her of her attachments. Keats had no one.

"I suppose you'll have to find someone else now," she said to keep the conversation moving.

"Yes." He seemed surprised by the comment. "I have someone in mind."

With his secret safely locked in her consciousness, she no longer feared what he might say. Lieutenant Davis came into the breakroom. His eyes were slightly sunken from the predicted headache, but he smiled at them and moved quickly.

"I'm afraid you may have to stay in here a little longer. Jason's body is missing, again."

He calmly poured himself a cup of coffee.

Keats jumped out of his chair. "What happened?"

"We're not sure. Sergeant Harris went to check the lab. He found Checkers on the floor unconscious, but no sign of Jason's body. And now we're not sure who was with Checkers."

"How's Checkers?" asked Clara, holding her breath.

"Fine. No idea what happened. He remembers pushing the stretcher into the lab then says everything went black. Medic says he's fine." Lieutenant Davis opened the door to leave then added, "I'll check in with you when I know something."

Clara moved to look out the window. She breathed a sigh of relief then realized it had been audible. Keats's reflection in the dark window told her he had heard it. He studied her.

"If you know where Avery or any of these others are, you should tell us." Keats had her secret. "These are killers you're protecting."

"I don't know where Avery is."

She didn't need emotional detachment to deal with Keats. Her emotions would keep Keats from finding out anything from her.

"They'll keep killing until we're all dead." He grabbed her shoulder and turned her around. "Don't you get it?"

Clara grabbed his hand and pushed him back. Her physical strength always surprised people. "I get it better than you do, Doctor." She turned back to look out the window. "And don't ever touch me again."

Keats recovered quickly from the shock of Clara's show of strength. "I saw you watching them take the body away. I thought you were just in shock, but you *knew* the body would go missing, just like you knew to bring the machete. You came here tonight intending to kill Jason."

"I always thought the stories Mama told me when I was growing up were just stories, but I listened. You should have."

"You're as mad as Jason." Keats threw his arms in the air and sat down. "You're willing to take old wives' tales to heart and ignore everything I'm trying to do."

"What are you trying to do?"

"What would it mean to the parents of a victim of a drunk driver to see their child heal quickly and go back to school with no long-term disability? What would it mean to a cancer patient to have that cancer gone without the agony of chemical and radiation therapy? The potential benefits are enormous, not to mention the ways added strength and keener senses could improve our daily lives."

"What about the price? Nothing in this world is free. Jason and the others pay a price for their so-called enhancements."

"Unless you help me now, I'll never be able to help either them or us."

"You don't want to help anyone. You live on glory. You want to be the one to tell this story."

"I thought you were a woman of intelligence, Dr. Lucas. Are you really willing to let superstition stand in the way of your better judgment?"

Clara wished she had told John about Max, to make him understand why she had come to the hospital tonight. She wanted the killing to stop but understood the killing would never cease. Healing people was a good thing, but at what price? She wondered if John would pay the price. Her head began to ache. She had to live with her decision now.

Looking down to the streets below, she watched the cars driving up and down the Seawall. Near the foot of the towers, summer students made their way to and from the library in preparation for summer midterms. Another group of white-coated students walked beneath her on their way into the hospital. Behind them, beyond the glow of the streetlights, someone stood so still that Clara noticed the stillness before noticing the figure. She thought the figure looked up at her. The form was familiar and horrific at the same time. *What was so familiar about it, and why am I so afraid?*

The door opened and John came in. "We're leaving," he said. "I've arranged for a plane to meet us at the airfield."

Clara looked again, but the figure had vanished.

"Clara?"

John came up beside Clara and looked out the window.

"Yes. I'm ready."

"Taking her along will only endanger the rest of us, Colonel," said Keats, still steaming. "I'm sure she's working with them."

"I'll decide who does and does not go with us."

Clara looked at John and realized how well he understood her.

"I have a project to salvage, Colonel," exclaimed Keats.

"I'm doing what I can, Doctor. You have ten minutes to get what you need from your office."

Clara looked into John's face and saw the colonel's face. He would do the right thing.

"Colonel Dietrich didn't have the types of problems you seem to be having. Perhaps I should call him and have him arrange the transport," said Keats, still unsatisfied with John's responses.

"Colonel Dietrich is dead." John looked directly at Clara. "They found his body early this morning in his car. It had been torched with him inside it."

Clara understood John's motives now better than she ever had. He risked his own life as his duty, but he would not risk hers.

"I can be of more use here —" began Keats.

"The next time they attack, they're coming for you, Keats."

The anger in John's voice reverberated silently in the room. Clara had never seen him so full of anger, and the quietness he assumed made him all the more frightening.

"You don't know that."

"They've been destroying the physical evidence of this project bit by bit. You're it. They get you and the project is dead. You now have nine minutes to get your things together."

John walked out of the room before Keats could reply.

* * * * *

Celia sat on the couch across from Reverend Brown in the recreation center. Madeline brought her a cup of tea and sat beside her.

"Thank you," said Celia as she breathed in fresh green fields, honey-dew, and mountain mist.

She loved her green tea, and the odd-looking woman with Reverend Brown made the perfect cup. Celia examined the details of Madeline. *Perhaps odd isn't the right word.* Her face contained traces of Asia, but her frame and coloring were a decidedly Caucasian and African mix. Madeline's dress fit her full frame perfectly, but its cut reminded Celia of the dresses her grandmother wore. Large, colorful flowers filled a black field; orange floral earrings accented the unusual coloring of her skin; and her dark hair wound itself with twists and curls into a neat bun on the nape of her neck.

Reverend Brown introduced Madeline as Sister Madeline. Celia assumed he meant a sister in the church, but she wondered if they could actually be brother and sister. While Celia first thought Madeline looked odd, her first impression of Reverend Brown was striking. He stood at least as tall as her late husband, but where her husband prided himself on being fit and ripped, the reverend's Polynesian ancestry reverberated from within, rounding out to fill his navy blue suit. This worked with instead of contrasting with his African heritage. His dark skin glowed on his Asian face. Only the wide, flat mustache seemed out of place on his handsome face.

"You're an amazing woman, Mrs. Haskins." Even the reverend's voice perfectly fit his appearance. It sang instead of lectured in a deep, mellow tone. "When your son said you had come here to help, I knew I was about to meet an extraordinary woman."

Despite the charms of Reverend Brown, Celia kept him at a distance. She did not survive as a Sergeant Major's wife without spotting imposters and con artists looking for easy military marks.

"None of us here today know who died in the explosion this morning. A little later today," Celia looked in the direction of a group of men and women gathered near the television, "some of them will soon be joining me in burying their loved ones. They need me here as much as I need to be here."

Celia felt tears forming in her eyes, again. She drank her tea. Madeline's hand on her shoulder didn't seem like a con. There were cons out there good enough to fool most, but when Celia looked up, she didn't see the expected tears in Madeline's eyes. She saw someone who understood her pain.

"Indeed, Mrs. Haskins. This is where you belong. And we will not intrude on your grief. We came only to help."

Reverend Brown stared out the window behind Celia. "We've only been in Los Angeles for a few days. When I saw the news about what happened to your husband, a man so decorated and so tragically taken, I felt I had to do something. Sister Madeline is a certified grief counselor, and I've worked with many families in their time of need. We do not charge any money. Our ministry is well endowed. In fact, if we may, we would like to help with funeral expenses. These poor people have more important things to worry about than money. And of course, I offer my services for free."

"That's very kind, reverend. Most of those missing have young families."

Celia wanted to believe in the sincerity of the reverend and his friend.

When Kate Black, Captain Black's wife, rang the doorbell at Celia's house this morning, she intended only to deliver a couple of casseroles. Celia had woken in the early morning hours to the sound of the explosion but could get no answers from anyone about what happened. Kate explained that the restricted labs had exploded and that there were a number of missing soldiers and civilians. To add to the confusion and complication, Colonel Deitrich's car was found not far from the main gates. It too had exploded. The colonel had died instantly. Kate was on her way to the recreation center to help organize the families of the missing. Celia had not hesitated to volunteer.

Kate Black demanded and received respect when she entered a room, but her efficiency wasn't with people. Celia took care of the people while Kate organized the recreation center and supplies. Captain Hill's friend arrived shortly after Kate and Celia. She worked wonders with children. Lizzie took them all into one of the craft rooms and had them playing games while their parents paced, cried, and bit their nails. Celia might not like Lizzie very much, but she admitted that she was useful.

Celia had noticed the arrival of Reverend Brown as soon as he entered the room. She hadn't noticed when Madeline arrived or when she took over organizing coffee, tea, and sandwiches to everyone. Sister Madeline moved around a crowd as unnoticed as everyone else.

"You said you went to my house looking for me, Reverend," said Celia.

"Yes, we did. As I said, I heard about your husband and wanted to offer my assistance. Your son filled us in on what happened last night. We just had to come to help anyway we could."

The reverend must have a way with people. Dorian doesn't talk to anyone.

"Perhaps you can stay around just a little longer."

Celia noticed the Base Commander entering the recreation center. The army Chaplin and that new Lieutenant Diggers she didn't know much about was with him. Celia stood to follow them. Reverend Brown and Sister Madeline stood, too, with the reverend prepared to lead the way. The lieutenant nodded his head in recognition to them. *So, the reverend isn't just here out of goodness.*

9

Beyond the crowded streets where youthful revelers parade and toast the summer's heat, where iron birds perch and roar and frighten songbirds into silence, a man walks alone beside the road with a brown paper bag for a friend. From his belt, a long, thin line to his ears whispers a voice of comfort that eases his soul as the bottle in the bag eases his tired bones. He stumbles in the grass. The bottle breaks on the pavement. The night breeze covers him with mist as a summer shower dusts the fields around him. His curses fall on sharpened ears. A car passes by. He follows its headlights and catches the glimmer of green orbs in the grass. Somewhere nearby, a woman sits in a chair watching the distant lights of a storm flash over the water. She waits for her man, but he never comes home.

What watches in the shadows
when you walk alone?
Where sea and shore battle
seems a fitting place
to end the debate between night and day.
Whisper, and hear the beating of wings.
Sing loud and hear the angels cry.
Let Mary Midnight guide you,
as I always do, from KMND Galveston.

Tonight, my children, we are each on our own,
unless we are together.
Victory waits to crown a victor.

Keats refused to budge before he collected all his papers, so it took another fifteen minutes to leave the hospital. But John anticipated this, so they weren't behind his schedule. He planned to make use of the extra time to talk to Clara. She eagerly told him about the visit from Max and about Tommy. The words rolled out of her mouth as though lives depended on her not taking a breath, which they did. The fact that she had hidden the information from him earlier didn't anger him. He wouldn't have believed her.

Even now he didn't want to believe her. Nothing about this assignment made logical sense. The only point that really upset him was Max. He wished that Clara had told him that Max was in the hospital. He let that slide since it proved that they wanted the physical evidence. John told Lieutenant Davis to upload all the data he had collected from the surveillance cameras directly to the Pentagon computers. If all went well, Keats and Clara would soon be off the island and in a secured facility.

On schedule, John ushered them into the back seat of a car. Corporal Checkers drove. John sat up front. He'd left enough guards at the hospital to keep the labs secure until the cleanup crew arrived. All the others loaded into the back of a truck to follow the car. Keats, obviously upset about leaving, remained silent either because he had talked too much earlier and his throat wouldn't let him, or because John in his full anger frightened him.

Clara remained remarkably calm. John pointed out to her that while Max may have promised to protect her, the vow did not spread to anyone else.

Once they left the hospital, things didn't go according to John's plan. A light rain began to fall as soon as they turned off the campus onto Broadway. Over the Gulf, lightning flashed and cracked as a storm moved slowly toward the island. The storm was still far away, but John worried that it would stop them from flying out. The drizzle soon let up, though, and John saw stars again. Old Victorian homes blocked his view of the water, but he caught telltale signs of lightning above their roofs.

Their drive down Broadway slowed to a crawl. Twice they had to wait for the police to stop the street dancing and put teens back in their cars. Cars stopping and occupants changing cars seemed to be a favorite pastime for the young tourists. They had to wait as two cars full of young men jumped out and started fighting. Then a traffic accident stopped them. Clara finally spoke up and directed Rodriquez to a back street that would take them the direction they wanted. Once off Broadway, they moved along easily.

John first became aware of someone following them as they turned off the congested boulevard. He'd expected the enemy to follow them, and on the quiet streets, motorcycle riders were easy to spot. First, he watched a lone motorcycle hanging back just far enough away not to threaten them. From time to time a new motorcycle replaced it. Sometimes he noticed one parked on a side street. That would start up as soon as they crossed an intersection. He remembered the motorcycles that night on the beach when he had watched Avery. She had met Max that night, not Jacob. There appeared to be a total of five bikes following them. Checkers kept checking the rearview mirror. He obviously saw them, too. Neither Keats nor Clara said anything. John supposed that they didn't notice.

Finally, they turned onto Stewart Road. The motorcycles didn't follow them, but they hadn't abandoned their hunt. The road curved at the formal entrance to Moody Gardens. John had always enjoyed the glimpse up the garden road that led to the great coral hotel with the three glass pyramids looming up behind it. But tonight, the lighted palm trees and flowering oleanders only concealed hiding places. Construction on Airport Drive meant they had to turn into the tourist garden. For just a moment, John lost sight of the truck. A construction sign turned them again, and both vehicles reunited on the road leading to the airport.

Moody Gardens continued stretching out on their right. The pyramids reached up toward the stars, and a small plane slowly made its way to the ground. They drove past the terminal to the end of the runway. They halted in front of an old hangar. No one got out of the car.

John looked toward the sky, and then at his watch. "Where the hell are they?" he said, more to himself than anyone else. He wiped the sweat from his brow. "Damn heat."

He stepped out of the car and motioned to the truck. Sergeant Harris led his soldiers out of the truck and began to scan the area, eager to be out of the confining space.

"John," said Clara, stepping out of the car.

"They should be here..." He stopped without finishing his sentence. The small plane they had seen landing sat in the middle of the runway, its engines off and the cockpit door open. "Harris!" he yelled. "Check it out."

Before Harris responded, they both turned their heads to the sounds of motorcycles coming toward them. John grabbed Clara and motioned Keats to follow. Checkers raced to the back of the car to pull something out of the trunk. John called on a nearby private and led them to the side door of the hanger. He tried the door once then used the butt of his shotgun to force it. A small office sat across from them on the opposite side of the hangar.

"Take them in there!" ordered John. He turned to go out, but Clara stopped him. "I have to go, Clara. Take this."

He handed her his handgun from his belt and left.

The motorcycles began circling them, moving closer and closer, but they had yet to reach any of his soldiers. The bikers were either hesitating or waiting, but they continued to creep closer in. John had to hold them off till the reinforcements and the plane arrived. He understood fighting, and in other circumstances he would have relished successfully drawing out his enemy. He looked to Harris and gave the order to start shooting. The noise of the shotguns and motorcycles immediately filled the night, deafening the sounds from Broadway.

No sooner did one motorcyclist fall from a gunshot than another took his place. John took a deep breath and pulled a long tube out of the backpack Checkers had just finished fastening to himself. He signaled Sergeant Harris, who did the same, and together they lit the tubes. Flames flew, catching the riders by surprise. There were screams and then explosions as gas tanks ignited, spilling fuel and flames. Barrels of fuel near the end of the hangar toppled over and poured out their contents, which also began to burn. But the riders still came.

John handed the flamethrower to a soldier and stepped back. Sergeant Harris had good control of his people. John looked at his watch and then at the sky. Through the smoke, he saw the pyramids and the stars. He had to fight to take Keats off the island, but this enemy seemed reluctant to fight. The motorcyclists continued to threaten but were being held off too easily. Finally, through the roar of battle, he heard the sound he wanted to hear. He looked up again and saw the lights of a helicopter coming closer. Following the helicopter would be the truck with the additional soldiers he would need to end the attack. And after that, he hoped, the plane would arrive.

Some of the bikers stopped and looked up. Most continued moving in. He followed the gaze of one of the motorcyclists back to the pyramids. John felt that pit in his stomach he always got when things were wrong. While he had looked at the pyramids before, he hadn't noticed the figures along the glass walls. Standing as though on flat ground were people, but people John didn't want to know. Suddenly he heard a scream as a young soldier was grabbed from behind. New attackers now leaped at his soldiers from the roof of the hangar. They jumped down as though it were only a step. John continued throwing flames and began shouting orders. Clara and Keats were in danger, but he could not get to them now.

*****

Keats clutched his briefcase to his chest as they ran across the hangar to the small office. Clara hung on to the handgun, despite knowing it wasn't the best protection. As they reached the office, they heard something fall to the floor.

"Quick!" whispered the private.

He opened the door, and they followed.

The only window opened into the darkened, mostly empty hangar. Clara reached for the desk and found a small lamp. The soldier crouched against the door with his back to her. Keats pulled out a chair and sat down as though in his own office. Clara watched him out of the corner of her eye. Despite his cool demeanor, he was restless and fidgeted in his seat. Her heart still pounded from the run and the fear. Her hair still stood up on her arms and neck. She bit her lip, wondering if she would survive this night. Of the three, only the soldier seemed unaffected by the fright and run across the hangar.

"I'm going to check things out," he said, and slowly began to open the door.

"You'd do better by staying here," said Keats.

His coarse voice didn't betray any fear.

"Keats!" Clara started to protest but stopped short.

The soldier slowly turned around. Clara saw the light reflecting in his eyes and a sneer turning up his lips. "If you insist." A long slow growl echoed from the back of his throat as he showed his long white teeth and prepared to lunge for Keats.

The creature lunged, and she shot it. The blast threw him against the door, slamming it shut. Before she could move, Keats pulled her machete out of his briefcase and in one slice took his head off.

"I was wondering what happened to that," said Clara.

Keats picked up a shirt hanging on a coat rack and cleaned the blood off the machete.

"I'm a quick learner, Dr. Lucas. I only thought to keep it as evidence, but ..." He stopped and looked around him. "Do you smell something?"

"Fire," she said.

They both moved toward the door. Keats waited for her to help him move the headless body.

*****

The hanger doors were slightly apart. Flames and smoke flowed into the building. At least the flames gave them light. They could make out the shapes of a few small planes and the door they had entered on the opposite wall. The sound of gunfire grew less now and seemed farther away. Clara stood still, trying to decide what to do when her eyes finally focused on some barrels near the large doors.

"We better get out of here," she said, and started to walk out.

Keats grabbed her arm. "What are you thinking? We don't know what's happening out there."

She pointed to the open doors. "But I know what's going to happen here if those flames get too close to those barrels."

Clara led the way out of the office slowly. She watched every shadow as though it had eyes and looked back at her. Halfway through the hangar, she felt herself relax, then resumed her vigilance, afraid that relaxing might send signals to their attackers. Keats moved up beside her so close that she could smell his sweat. They were almost to the door and began to hurry when the door suddenly opened. Clara pointed the shotgun instantly.

"Clara!" shouted John.

She almost dropped the weapon.

"What happened?" asked Keats.

"Reinforcements arrived and they're running,"

John spoke quickly and calmly.

He moved up and took Clara's arm to lead her out while also taking her gun.

"You're not afraid of a few little flames are you, Ms. Clara?"

Clara knew that voice well. She turned quickly. Tommy sat on the wing of a small plane, stretched out as though watching television. He leapt off the wing and walked toward them. John pulled on her arm then stopped. Behind her, others stood just within the shadows, out of view, but within sight. The small door closed.

Tommy moved toward them slowly, his golden curls dancing in the firelight. He wore a dark, fitted suit and shirt. Clara decided that her favorite sacker had seen too many vampire movies.

"Ms. Clara, I'm surprised at you, hanging out with such violent people."

"I could say the same about you," she replied, pushing the lump out of her throat.

Tommy unleashed that cherub smile he had mastered so well. "Hardly surprising considering the swamp trash you come from. Do you really think your friends can stop us from killing all of you?"

"I'll make sure we get you before we die." John used his stone, colonel's voice that made those around him stand straight and listen.

Clara wondered how that voice took the fear out of her. Anger replaced it. A hissing pop grabbed her attention as Sergeant Harris, in one motion, pulled out the tube of a flamethrower and lit it.

Tommy didn't step back, but his smile became mean and less boyish. "You have no idea what you're up against, Colonel. I haven't lived this long by being afraid of little men with toys."

John smiled. "If you're so smart, why don't you get this over with?"

Clara stared intently at Tommy. His expression remained the same but thoughts raced across his face.

"Now, Ms. Clara, you don't want this, do you? We can all be reasonable about this. All we want is him." Tommy pointed to Keats.

"What guarantee do we get that if we hand him over you won't change your mind?"

Clara saw a satisfied smirk race across Tommy's face as John spoke and wondered what John was planning.

"Colonel!" shouted Keats.

For the first time, Clara heard fear in his voice.

"Shut up, Keats."

John didn't take his eyes off Thomas.

"I won't." Keats turned to Thomas. "It doesn't have to be this way. I learned a great deal from Jason. In time, I can cure you."

"Cure me?" laughed Tommy.

He laughed so hard he had to step back. Just as he appeared so young and innocent, his laughter sang sweet and pure. It echoed throughout the hangar, drowning out the sound of rage around them. Clara suddenly realized the figures standing around them were whispering to each other. Some laughed with Tommy, but the sound floated around them like a whisper across the lake almost out of range of hearing.

"What makes you think there is anything to cure me of?"

Keats stood still with nothing to say. His face betrayed the disgust and fear he felt. "You can't want to be this way."

Tommy stopped laughing as suddenly as he had started. His eyes burned brighter than the flames in the hanger. "You killed Jason."

"Listen to reason," started Keats. "I know what went wrong with Jason."

"Keats!" shouted John.

He reached forward to pull Keats back, but Tommy stepped forward. Instead of grabbing for Keats, Tommy pushed him into John. The force sent both Keats and John crashing to the floor. The shotgun fell out of John's hand, and he landed on his right arm. Clara heard a loud crack as his arm broke. She had to step back to avoid falling with them. Tommy made his move and pulled Clara to him.

"What do you think, Colonel?" asked Tommy.

Clara tried to move, but it was like trying to move stone. He held her head back on his shoulder and one arm behind her back. She wondered why she had never noticed that he had such sharp white teeth.

"Fair trade?"

She took in everything around her. Behind John and the others, she could see shadowy figures begin to move forward. A bright orange flame flew toward them. One of the approaching figures suddenly screamed in pain and ran wild about the hangar. The others stopped. The flaming figure raced toward the hangar doors, knocking over several barrels.

Clara saw dark liquid seeping out. Soon the fuel oil would spread to the flames outside the hanger doors.

Clara closed her eyes and waited for Tommy to sink those sharp teeth into her neck. Instead, he suddenly pushed her away. She landed on the ground where John had dropped his shotgun. She picked it up and looked at him. The pain on his face instantly changed to relief as she reached for him. He looked up at Tommy, and she followed his gaze.

Max held Tommy up against the side of an airplane. "Why have I never bothered to kill you?"

"You don't have what it takes," growled Tommy with his hands around Max's throat.

Clara stood up, keeping the shotgun pointed at them. Keats helped John up.

"Are you all right?" she whispered.

He put his good hand on her shoulder. "Just keep that pointed at them."

"Face it, Max, you've lost your touch! You're pissed off because I got here first. Even your own people helped me get them here."

"You weren't supposed to start a war."

The whispering from the shadows stopped. The sudden silence caught Clara's attention. Even the sound of the fire died down. From behind the plane, Clara thought someone walked toward them. Avery never walked anywhere unless she had a purpose.

Clara found herself pointing the shotgun at her old friend. If Avery noticed, she made no sign of it. "If your dance cards aren't too full, I'd like to go before burning to a crisp."

Max suddenly let Tommy go, and they both stiffened like schoolboys before the principal.

Tommy turned to her. "You've got no say in this, woman. Stay out of what you don't understand."

"Please! Act your real age for once. Besides, I'm not making this call, sweetheart." Avery gave Tommy her best wolfish grin and pointed behind her. "He is."

Clara followed where Avery pointed. The large hangar doors opened wider filling the hanger with the red light of the flames. Someone stood there for a moment perfectly still, but then with no effort glided toward them. The tall, lean figure cast a long shadow that sent a chill into Clara, the same chill she had felt in Avery's office. Fear tightened its hand around her heart. She let the shotgun hang down. It would do no good against the force moving toward them now. John moaned slightly and held his right arm with his left hand. She moved closer to him. The flames from outside ignited the fuel oil on the ground inside the hanger with a flash.

"No one else has to die, John," said Avery, speaking a little faster than usual, but without losing her composure. She smiled as if she had simply walked in on a dinner party.

John took a deep breath and turned to face Avery. "What's the deal?"

"You walk away."

"What?" exclaimed Tommy.

"Aren't you in enough trouble?"

Avery glared back at him. Tommy looked up at the figure at the end of the hangar and said nothing more.

"If you're going to use that, Clara, you should hold it properly."

"She'll kill us if you don't use it," said Keats.

"Not now, Keats." John took a deep breath. Clara noticed the pain in his voice. "What's the catch?"

"No catch. Just walk away." Avery spoke to John but watched Clara.

Clara felt a shiver. The silhouetted man raised his hand. Harris swore as his flamethrower went out; he couldn't relight it. The shotgun suddenly weighed a ton and crashed to the ground.

"Guess you win," coughed John.

The smoke continued to thicken.

"Better to say a draw," said Avery with that same social smile. "What would be the point if either of us won?" Avery turned her attention to Keats. Her smile became that cold grin Clara had seen back at the hospital. "Don't worry, Keats, I know I promised to kill you, but I can't." She paused a moment before adding, "Tonight."

"I knew you were behind all of this." His voice was dry and bitterly threatening, which surprised Clara as he could do nothing to anyone given the immediate threat to them all.

"You know the rules," said Tommy excitedly, speaking to the man at the end of the hangar. "They killed Jason."

"Jason was mad," Max spoke calmly.

Tommy turned to say something to Max but stopped and stared at the mysterious man. The hangar grew brighter as the flames moved closer to the barrels. Through the smoke above the flames, Clara looked at the tallest of the pyramids lighted against the night sky. Despite the flames, the man at the end of the hangar didn't move. He lifted his arm again and pointed a long, white, crooked finger in her direction. The figure's head lifted for a moment, and Clara could just make out the same sickly pallor on the skin of his face. She was glad not to be able to see his features.

John saw the same thing and put his good arm around her. She looked to Avery for an explanation, but Avery neither moved nor changed expression.

"It's not my fault!" yelled Tommy. "I didn't do anything wrong!"

Clara realized the man pointed to Thomas, not her.

Whatever Clara witnessed unfolding that night would play out another time. A military truck ran through the flames and into the hangar. Soldiers jumped out firing.

"Get to the door," John said quickly in her ear.

He bent slightly, grabbing his broken arm, then turned toward his soldiers. Harris reached for Keats, but Thomas was faster and pushed Keats to the floor, grabbed his briefcase, then disappeared into the flames and smoke. Clara watched from the edge of the hangar as John ran to his soldiers, shouting orders. In the smoke and confusion, she lost sight of him and everybody else.

"I told them he was smarter than he looks."

Avery stood beside Clara. She took Clara's hand in hers. The heat of a burning hanger began burning into Clara's skin, making the coolness of Avery's comforting.

"You have to go." Clara tried covering her mouth and nose with her other hand to keep the smoke out. "They'll lock you up like they did Jason."

She followed Avery.

"I have to leave. That's the rule, but I wanted to say goodbye. Besides, after tonight, I imagine just about everybody will be leaving."

"Who was he?" Clara asked, nodding her head in the direction of the large hangar doors.

The smoked made it hard to see Avery. Her face reflected the orange glow of the flames, making Clara squint in the glare. But Clara knew that once clear of the building, Avery would go.

"You don't want to know. Besides, it doesn't matter now. What matters is getting you out of here."

Clara let it drop, remembering Max's warning. They reached the small side door.

"I'm going to miss you."

The sounds of battle diminished as the roar of the burning increased.

"I'll miss you too, but we all have our duties."

Clara noticed that she seemed unaffected by the smoke. They were only a few feet away from the door when Clara heard a shotgun blast close to her ear. Instinctively, she fell to the ground, pushing Avery with her.

She rolled to her side. Keats stood over Avery, pointing a shotgun at her head.

Clara grabbed her friend. "No!"

"Get out of the way," shouted Keats, suddenly finding his voice. Malice dripped from his every pore.

Clara looked at her friend's face but saw no fear, only her usual smile. Her eyes, however, spoke louder to Clara than any words could. They reflected the flames within the hanger and burned with a fire hotter than she had ever seen.

"Get out of the way, Dr. Lucas!" shouted Keats again.

Clara didn't move.

"Keats!" John tried to push Keats out of the way, but Keats used the butt of the gun as a hammer on John's broken arm.

John fell to the ground in pain.

"If you won't do your duty, I'll do it for you," Keats shouted.

Clara started to get up and go to John, but Avery grabbed her arm with an iron grip. Before Clara could object, Max appeared and threw Keats back into the hanger. Avery stood and pulled Clara up. The smoke began to choke her. Clara saw neither John nor Keats. She began coughing as breathing became difficult in the smoke.

"Fuses set. It's going to blow in another twenty seconds."

Clara heard Max but could no longer see him. Avery's cold hand led her away from the building. She wasn't sure when Avery let her go. Her coughing became too much for her to stand straight. Suddenly, someone else helped her to an ambulance and oxygen mask.

She looked behind her searching for John. She tried to go back toward the hanger but was pulled back. Then she saw Sergeant Harris carrying Keats, and John walking behind them, clutching his broken arm.

She sat in the back of the ambulance, breathing in oxygen as a medic checked her blood pressure. Her throat burned a little less now. The medic removed the oxygen mask and offered her a bottle of water. She greedily let the water wash the smoke from her mouth and cool the back of her throat. She wished she were at home.

Outside the truck, soldiers still searched the area. She knew they wouldn't find anything, and suspected John knew that as well. He stood next to the fire truck talking with the police chief. The police had arrived with the fire department. Clara watched John as he talked to the chief, feeding him what she assumed would be some story of a covert operation involving international terrorists. It was just the right kind of thing to leak to the press and keep the locals buzzing for a week, perhaps two if tourism slowed.

She worried about John, but he seemed fine. His right arm rested in a sling. At least the break seemed clean. She didn't argue with him when he told her to stay in the truck.

Keats had only a few cuts and bruises to boast of. He laughed as he talked about how Tommy took his briefcase and ran. "Nothing in it, you know. All my data is electronic and secure on Pentagon servers."

He boasted about how little the vampires had gained. Clara let his smugness roll off her. It would have irritated her the day before but not now. She looked hard into the surrounding shadows, wondering if Avery was watching. She couldn't help remembering Avery saying that she couldn't kill Keats, "tonight." Her friend had left, and for now, so had the danger to Keats. *Why not kill him tonight? And what was it Lieutenant Davis said about Avery installing a virus?*

Keats kept on talking, and Clara's thoughts wondered. *What was gained by all of this? Perhaps it was a draw.* Keats seemed to see it only as a setback in his research.

John walked away from the police chief. Fatigue drooped his shoulders, but his face remained grim. She wanted to get out of the truck and tell him to get to the doctor, but she didn't. He had too much thinking to do. *He gained an insight tonight he hadn't looked for and doesn't want.*

Clara leaned back and stared up at the stars. The great glass pyramids, still lighted, shone in the sky like neon beacons. Clara's eyes began to close. She tried focusing on the tallest of the pyramids and saw the figures, standing on it. She wondered how long they had been there and if Avery stood with them.

When John took her hand, she startled.

"Didn't mean to wake you," he said.

Despite his grim exterior, he was the same John she had fallen in love with.

"You need a doctor to set that arm," she said.

"I know. Just as soon as I know you're safe."

He waited as she got out of the truck and then led her to the car. As they drove away, she looked back at the pyramids and saw the figures silhouetted in the night sky.

"What will happen now?" she asked.

"There's one more thing I have to do."

"And then what?"

She suddenly realized John no longer had a reason to be on the island.

"I've been thinking about taking up fishing."

He smiled at her, and then he leaned his head back in the passenger seat and closed his eyes.

*****

On Pelican Island, among the tall grasses and brown pelicans, stands a cinder block building with blue neon letters above an open door. Crouching in the tall grass are men dressed in black, hiding their fears behind black masks. The wind shifts and a bird cries, the night is long and hot. A signal. Silent, stealthily they move. A sudden rush and they are in, but the room is empty. The aroma of coffee fills their nostrils. Cups are neatly stacked. The coffee is hot. Lights flicker green and red beyond the glass of the control room. But the room is dark. One man removes his mask and uses a long sheath of grass to scratch beneath the cast on his arm. He feels a cool breeze brush against his cheek. From the speakers comes the voice in the night. In the corner of his eye, out the door, beyond the blue neon above the door, a figure or a shadow flutters away.

Ah, my children, the moon shines upon us.
Drink in the flavor of another night.
Let all the day be gone and past.
The night is our dream, and our truth,
and all that is.
Let the sun blind those who will not see.
Victory, store your crown away,
no prince will come to claim that prize,
not this night, not yet.
At last Mary Midnight must bid adieu
to her children here in Galveston.
A guard stands where once there was none.
He has not come to rule.
He knows the price Victory demands.
And he knows what you find

when you go hunting shadows.

About the L.K. Latham

L.K. Latham writes Urban Fantasy and poetry that's about as dark as the chocolate she loves. She spends her days weaving tales of vampires, werewolves, and other creatures known to Dance in the Shadows of the Moon. When not writing, you'll find L.K. baking with chocolate and wine. In the evenings, she rests with a class of bourbon - made in Texas, of course, and waiting for last year's grapes to become this year's wine.

A recovering educator, this native Texas settled in the Austin area with her husband. She enjoys living in Texas as much as she enjoys the wines of Texas, perhaps a bit more than some of its inhabitants, but that doesn't stop her from admiring their spunk and veracity in the face of overwhelming facts.

Visit L.K. at https://lklatham.com and sign up for her newsletter to recieve updates on her latest books and free short stories.

Midnight Loyalties

Find out where Mary Midnight goes next in *Midnight Loyalties*.

The pool closed an hour ago. The alumnus hosting the party paid for the bar to stay open until ten o'clock. After that, the players, the players' girlfriends, the players' friends, and the players' hangers-on left. The non-players stayed another half hour to be polite. By then, the alum had grown tired, and the faculty had eaten the last of the food. All were ready to go home after a successful back-to-school welcome party for the football team. The staff removed the remnants of the party and turned out the lights, but the mirth and life on Fifth Street continued to sprinkle life on the rooftop lounge.

Harry crouched on the ledge above the pool, surveying his city, remembering when dust floated from the scuffle of young male collegiates gathering on street corners, when small town politicians hustled between homes and brothels to make names for themselves in the burgeoning capital, and when visions of a rose-colored dome dominating the city first took flight in the dreams of visionaries. He remembered the lovely ladies of old Pecan Street dancing under the red lights, and he remembered the hate and the apathy for those who were not wanted but were always needed. Tonight, he listened to the blues swelling out of Antone's mingle with the jazz, rock, and country music floating in the breezes from Fifth Street as new adults drank with newfound freedoms and pressures to excel and experienced the joy of independence. He grinned. In the morning, they'll experience the crush of reality as headaches and cotton mouth trap them behind doors in tiled palaces. The lotus of lights crowning the cityscape glowed, unchanged by the revelry below. Everywhere, the lights and sounds of Austin exhaled. Life flowed through its streets as blood through its veins. And mixing with the booze, food, piss, and smoke rose the essence of being. The hairs in his nose twitched with excitement.

Above the den of youth and life, he remembered lives long gone and lives budding new. Her voice echoed past and future, calmed souls, and sent bedlam and mirth stirring. He smiled to hear the voice flowing with the life of the city.

Tonight begins again, what long ago was.
Walk into the future with eyes opened to the past.
Let not the dreams of dawn hinder shadows crossing in the night.
For upon my brow the glittering night crowns what my eyes claim.
Fear not the passing of the day, but welcome moonshine's blinding rays.
Dance the dance of life and love.
Where my voice lingers, warriors gather for the fight.
Death walks your streets tonight.
Live or die, I will always be.
You're listening to Mary Midnight, online and in your mind.
Will Austin be the city of night or the dream of what was?

She arrived as shadow to stand beside him. He reached his hand, frail, white, and strong to hers. She placed fingers paler than age into his palm, allowing him to move her hand close to his lips.

"How I have missed you, my truest friend." He kissed fingers glazed with long red nails but no embellishments and gazed into the depths of eyes pale-black, deep, and knowing.

"If I hadn't stayed away..." Her voice sang the saddest of music but faded away as her gaze turned to the life below.

"Don't be sad. It's time, and there is no one I would rather leave this to. I like your new name. It suits you, but you'll always be my Duchess."

"Names change." Her voice, always smooth, flowing, commanding whispered in his ears. "Our hearts remain unchained."

They walked hand in hand along the streets and alleys of the city saying nothing, observing, breathing in the essence of its life.

The revelry of the young gave way to the realities of life. Two men with long hair and beards stirred against the cool concrete on the veranda of the Long Center. A German Shepard pup nuzzled close to the older of the men. Neither was old nor young, only lost and hungry. One woke but did not see the shadow of the couple standing above them, gazing at the city reflected in the slow-flowing river.

"Are you certain?" Her voice floated on the first breeze of dawn as it slipped around them, though the sun was still far away.

"Yes. I would never have let them disturb you as they did when I was young. I've lost touch."

"Once, no one would have dared challenge even your name, but the young today have different ideas. We grow with the times, or we fade."

"Thus will you survive." He kissed her hand, held it close to his chest. "I'm so sorry about this summer—"

"Don't!" she interrupted. "We all underestimated them, but I left the city once again in balance."

"And you will set it right here, once I am gone. War is upon us."

"Live just a little longer, my dearest. Love, one more time. Leave us all the richer for having you among us."

She kissed his cheek before turning her gaze to the drowsy man and his sleeping partner. "Dinner?"

www.ingramcontent.com/pod-product-compliance
Lightning Source LLC
Chambersburg PA
CBHW060453300726
48975CB00008B/2501